Stepping Off

The C

L. J. Cluskey

All loved ones,

All souls of the RMS Titanic,

All souls of the RMS Carpathia.

- Introduction -

Chapter 1 – Survivors of Titanic

Chapter 2 – Congressional Investigations

Chapter 3 – World War I, the Britannic and the Lusitania

Chapter 4 – The Olympic Troop Ship

Chapter 5 – The End of an Era

Chapter 6 – The Move to Massachusetts

Chapter 7 – The Meeting of Ruben Edwards, John Albert and Francesca Draycott

Chapter 8 – Moving Back to New York

Chapter 9 – Poets of New York

Chapter 10 – The Emergence of Benjamin Hartley

Chapter 11 – A Night Out to Remember

Chapter 12 – Benjamin Hartley and Archie Knox meet Al Capone

Chapter 13 – Mid–town, Broadway, Manhattan

Chapter 14 – The Quests of Those Involved

Chapter 15 – The Car Chase to New York Harbour through to the Boats

Chapter 16 – New York Hospital

Chapter 17 – The Handing Over and the End of the Road

Chapter 18 – Back in Massachusetts

Chapter 19 – The Ending of Stepping off the Carpathia

Introduction

Let me begin by saying before starting this writing campaign I thought many creative achievements had been written over the years on the subject of rescue ship RMS Carpathia and RMS Titanic, so initially there was the challenge for me as a writer to deliver the creative magnitude associated with these two transatlantic ocean liners. Thankfully, as challenging as this sea to land story is, I have managed to complete the narrative as an author.

You could say there is nowhere to go with this concept of a story because the other writings regarding these two historic ships have been completed to such a decent standard. However, here is the story in this book! I have to thank everyone who has been part of the creative accomplishments in being an inspiration to me when writing this book. The number of accolades and recognitions achieved throughout history symbolises the whole quality of a cultural experience for everyone concerned, with regards to the impact this influential but tragic story has had on people's lives in captivating their imagination regarding RMS Carpathia and RMS Titanic.

Now I have to introduce my writing and say this original story can follow the success on the subject of these two ocean liners regarding this creative magnitude required, as its own symbolic story titled 'Stepping off the Carpathia.' I simply thought of the idea through looking at an advertisement for a short story contest requiring me to write a two thousand five hundred word manuscript. As I started to think about what story I could write, there was only one winner.

Francesca Draycott is the descendant of English and Italian ancestors and has a destiny upon visiting family and old friends when over in Italy that requires her to complete a quest. She is asked by missionaries when in Rome to travel to America where she will eventually be contacted by other missionaries in the future regarding what she has been asked.

By chance she decides to travel to America on board RMS Titanic with her mother and father, Vivienne and Humphrey Draycott who are aware of what has been requested. Also with her is fiancé George Edwards who is aware of what the situation is. Mysteriously before the Titanic sails Francesca Draycott is offered the chance to sail on board the Mauretania instead at an earlier sailing date due to the 1912 coal strike.

After all four passengers dramatically survive the Titanic disaster they continue on their quest as RMS Carpathia docks in New York City. Eventually there is a move of residency to Boston, Massachusetts and back again to New York where other individuals are destined to meet Francesca Draycott as well as old adversaries in a fascinating tale!

Many Thanks

L. J. Cluskey

Stepping Off The Carpathia

-Chapter 1-

Survivors of Titanic

RMS Carpathia has docked at New York harbour where the rescue of those who managed to survive the sinking of RMS Titanic is complete. One of those survivors is a young lady named Francesca Draycott. In the commotion of making her way towards the ships exit door she manages to name herself to one of the steward's taking names of passengers departing the ocean liner. After stepping off the Carpathia on her own she is reunited with her mother and father in the pouring rain at the White Star Line registration point for surviving passengers, where a few moments later she notices her fiancé George Edwards as they embrace one another. He has also survived the Titanic disaster. This is an intensely emotional moment after what has happened on the ship's transatlantic maiden voyage across the Atlantic Ocean as their quest continues! Captain Arthur Rostron, his dedicated crew and passenger liner the RMS Carpathia have completed their heroic rescue mission.

Various survivors of the Titanic assembled in New York now have to face the facts they somehow have a life to live after surviving this maritime disaster. One of those individuals is J. Bruce Ismay, who is partly responsible for the sinking of Titanic; he is now making his way past the waiting assembled journalists. After ignoring a barrage of questions demanding answers as to why the Titanic is not docked there in front of them, Ismay turns away, disinterested. He looks like he is extremely disappointed and walks off after not saying anything. Privately, Ismay is a man haunted by what he knows he is responsible for and the path is now set for him to eventually deteriorate into private insanity.

He is also aware in the coming weeks and months he is going to have to attend a number of hearings regarding the Titanic disaster, where J. Bruce Ismay could be assumed solely responsible for what has happened in the North Atlantic and it is this accusation he is going to have to face during these hearings. After being vaguely informed there will be congressional investigations into the Titanic sinking by a White Star Line representative as he makes his way through the pack of hound's atmosphere at the harbour, Ismay again looks detached from the communication taking place. He looks as though he would be better off on the other side of the universe considering some of the questions he is being asked. This is compounded by the fact he was the one who put pressure on Captain Edward J. Smith to light the last boiler. In doing so, it meant the Titanic was travelling too fast at the moment when the ocean liner needed to steer clear of the iceberg with which it collided.

There is a slight air of optimism amongst the not-so-wealthy passengers having made it to New York and survived the disaster as they now have an opportunity to make things happen for themselves in their lives. They have moved to a new land where many nationalities are fulfilling their dreams of a better life and existence; destiny with hope can now be set for them. There is talk of going on from survival after the disaster and making new beginnings right across America.

Some passengers have been taken to a nearby makeshift hospital area in an office building having been transformed into a life-saving survival unit, with the people of New York helping them as much as they can in the empathy of the whole experience. People here are being kept alive with the most basic of food and drink but they have a truly gracious appreciation of this considering the experiences of almost the past three days. The main casualties are those survivors suffering from hyperthermia. Some casualties have a number of other injuries received out at sea during the sinking. Their recovery is underway and these people hope to be back on track, even though most of them have nothing left apart from their resilient spirit!

Meanwhile, two officers who were working on Titanic when the call came through from the watchtower are having a conversation at the front of the harbour looking out to New York Bay with one of them saying.

'I'm tendering my resignation when I get back to Southampton.'

This maybe symbolise the guilt many of the survivors of the disaster are already feeling as they seem to be questioning why they are still alive. This coincides with the thought of resignation of the officer who worked on the ship's bridge; he has now decided, once he has returned home to Southampton, his employment will be complete as far as maritime employment goes. With psychological replays in the minds of these two officers, you can understand why there is a presence of guilt concerning the disaster with memories of watching Titanic break in half itself. There is also the dreadful memory of the sound of the ship's metal creaking in leading up to the ocean liner disappearing into the sea and sinking they both cannot forget about as well.

One of these officers that has survived the disaster after manning Titanic's bridge is Charles Lightoller. As the evacuation of the ship began, he was one of the crew members in charge of loading the ship's passengers into lifeboats. Lightoller had received the Captain's orders of 'women and children first' where he pursued this principle in a military-like fashion. He and other officers also managed the situation to extend this procedure to mean 'women and children only.' In hindsight, he should not have done this considering it was not the actual order given by Captain Edward J. Smith.

Following this principle, Lightoller lowered lifeboats with empty seats even if there were no women or children waiting to board. To make his evacuation procedure even more specific, he permitted one solitary male passenger to board a lifeboat, namely Arthur Godfrey Peuchen, who was directed to depart in lifeboat six. He had enthusiastically informed the officer of his sailing experience and told him he would help navigate the boat coincidently full of women. Lightoller looked at him in a surprised manner as he calmly permitted him to board the lifeboat. Charles Lightoller stayed on board until the end, where in the drag of the ship's sinking, he was sucked against the grate of one of Titanic's funnels and held until he was underwater; at this point he was tragically on his way to the bottom of the Atlantic with the ocean liner. Dramatically, in being extremely lucky, he was blown from the grate by a rush of warm air as a boiler exploded. After this he managed to cling to a capsized collapsible lifeboat with thirty other gallant survivors as they waited to be rescued.

As Lightoller is looking out to New York harbour, his colleague and fellow officer looks at him, where he says inquisitively.

'How did you escape in the impact of Titanic's last moments when the funnel pulled you under?'

Charles Lightoller responds rather reflectively in remembering his escape from the ocean.

'Yes, I remember the moment. I honestly thought that was it because the force of the water pulled me into the drag of the Titanic sinking in relation to the funnel, ultimately the ocean. Then the next thing I knew there was this moment of luck with a blast of warm air after the explosion of the boiler.' He continues. 'It happened rather quickly to be honest regarding where the passengers were in correlation to the ship sinking and the distance they were sent on impact out in the direction of the escaping lifeboats, concerning Titanic's drag pulling them under as well.' Charles Lightoller responding rather reflectively in remembering his escape from the ocean.

The officer is listening with great interest as he looks at Lightoller and responds.

'You had one great but lucky escape at the same time considering your situation and the other passengers. The good old funnel came to the rescue! Sounds more like something out of a novel or the theatre!'

'Yes, I guess it was. I thought it was the luckiest moment of my life, particularly how we were catapulted out towards the escaping lifeboats! How about your escape?' Lightoller inquires.

His colleague looks out to the harbour as well as he starts to remember his escape

'Well, mine was slightly different to be honest. As far as I was aware, with the ship's evacuation procedure I, as the commanding officer of the last departing lifeboat, was supposed to board the lifeboat as well. It was the last lifeboat I was about to lower into the ocean, therefore I stepped off Titanic and continued my command into the lifeboat. There was a rather calm atmosphere on deck as I made my last calls for the lifeboat having women, children and men on board. There was no one left on the deck and the lifeboat was not completely full either, even though there were many passengers still on board the other decks at the same time.'

At this moment, Lightoller looks at him in a rather surprised way and asks.

'Well I never, I did not know you could evacuate as you did. I thought you had to stay on board the ship. Is that not the official procedure?'

'No, that is not the correct evacuation of the ship, as long as there are 'no women and children' still present within the vicinity of that particular part of the deck, you have to board that lifeboat.' The fellow officer replies. As the conversation is now becoming even more enlightening regarding the ship's evacuation procedure, the officer continues. 'Yes and you must preferably have a male passenger that you have permitted to command the particular lifeboat upon being lowered into the ocean. With Lightoller now looking a bit confused as to how he had commanded his evacuation of passengers, he responds.

'I was always under the impression you could not allow men to board the lifeboats and it was the captain's orders to allow 'women and children only' into the lifeboats.'

'No, there is a slightly different way of conducting an evacuation of a passenger liner in the middle of the ocean', his colleague informs him.

With Charles Lightoller now experiencing a realisation more men should have departed Titanic via the lifeboats he was commanding, responds by saying.

'Maybe I should pack it in as well when we return to Southampton.'

'Come on; let's get back to the hospital ward. There'll be people needing help.' Fellow officer Henry Morgans implies.

In the aftermath of the Titanic disaster, everyone concerned is wondering if some of the officers involved in the evacuation procedure completely misunderstood Captain Smith's instructions to load 'women and children first' into the lifeboats when many of the officers instructions were 'women and children only' with the lowering of some particular boats. There is a bizarre atmosphere among the survivors when discussing the evacuation of Titanic as to whether or not the loading of lifeboats was correct in the sense male passengers were left standing on the deck, when there were no 'women or children' waiting to board departing boats from any particular part of the deck and ship.

The general consensus is that under intense pressure concerning the presence of people waiting to evacuate the ship, some of the officers mistakenly took it on their own shoulders to call 'women and children only' instead of 'women and children first' as the lowering of lifeboats began. This is one factor now going to be considered during all Titanic investigations upon being administered, as to why so many people died in the North Atlantic Ocean.

-Chapter 2-

Congressional Investigations

After arriving in New York City, J. Bruce Ismay is almost immediately being informed of the congressional investigations hearing scheduled for the following day. When being told about the hearing he is once again despondent with what is trying to be communicated to him. He looks at the representatives from the authorities as if they are some sort of invisible messengers who are informing him of the situation. Just like with the waiting press at the harbour earlier in the evening, he takes a look at them, looks away and walks off after not saying anything. At this point Ismay's wife says politely to the representatives.

'Don't worry, he will definitely be there. He is just immensely shocked by what has happened and he is struggling to come to terms with everything. He is finding communicating with people extremely hard at the moment, so please do not take this personally. He will be at the hearing tomorrow.'

'Good to hear. There are quite a few people who have got a few questions for him. Hopefully he can speak! Thank you.' One of the representatives replies. Looking at Ismay's wife rather bemused. After this the representatives make their way towards the exit of the makeshift hospital and depart in a waiting car.

The following morning arrives in New York with an air of devastation descended onto the city concerning the Titanic disaster; the whole coverage of the disaster is still being covered daily in the New York press and the journalists covering the congressional investigations are assembling upon the building many witnesses are scheduled to attend, including a certain J Bruce Ismay and his wife. There is an instant air of pandemonium following the arrival of the Titanic survivors in New York. This urgent hearing, in the form of the congressional investigations, has been arranged literally as soon as it possibly could be, so the authorities can immediately question the people they need to and call on the required Titanic passengers to try and give as many answers as they can regarding what happened to Titanic.

The hearing has been arranged quickly because events will be as fresh in the minds of as many people as possible, considering the impact of the disaster on their memories. There is a certain individual who is extremely lucky to be attending the congressional investigations and this individual is. J Bruce Is may who they could say was partly, if not fully responsible for the Titanic disaster.

The morning has arrived for Ismay. He has awoken with his wife in a hotel room not far from where the hearing is to be held. They managed to find a place to stay quite late in the evening. Having to attend this hearing so soon after the Carpathia docking has docked in New York City is really not the best timing considering the fact Ismay appears to have lost the power of speech occasionally. If not, he has decided he chooses to speak to who he can be bothered speaking to after unduly managing to get to a lifeboat on the night of the Titanic disaster. Ismay is now seated in his hotel armchair looking out of the window. He turns to his wife and says.

'What is the point?' His wife looks surprised upon his comment and walks over to him.

'What on earth are you talking about Bruce? Are you talking about these congressional investigations? If you are, you now have to face up to it and attend this.'

'I am pleased to hear what they are called. I had no idea to be honest.' As he looks up at her from where is seated.

'Come along now; let's get ready to attend this hearing.' She says.

The intensity of the questioning is going to place a number of people under pressure and there is an element of it being too soon after arriving in New York to question everyone concerned. However, the authorities and people concerned decided the immediate congressional hearings had to take place, because the happenings on board Titanic are hopefully clearly remembered to a decent standard by everyone concerned. They had no other choice but to schedule the investigations as soon as they could because of the hopeful expectancy on those concerned for answers, as well as the waiting world media, interested to know what has happened, if not what went wrong, where and when.

The congressional investigations committee has been assembled hastily with various members being called from the relevant departments including government representatives, considering the high profile nature of the hearings. A schedule has been placed outside the room of the hearing and is now, in essence, a makeshift tribunal where the investigators concerned will have their opportunity to at least find some answers. Most importantly, for the passengers families who are still awaiting the news, in being informed what has actually happened in the North Atlantic. It is not surprising to all those looking at the schedule outside the room of the hearing a certain Mr J. Bruce Ismay is at the top of the schedule list for the day. The waiting journalists know who they want to question first when waiting for the individuals concerned to arrive outside this historic and fine architectural looking building; it will be the Ismay car approaching!

The black and beige coloured, spoke wheeled car pulls up! Bruce Ismay and his wife are inside. The waiting journalists assembled at the entrance area of the building are more like a pack of deranged lunatics. The car completely stops, thankfully for the Ismays precisely in front of the open door to the congressional investigations building. There is a barrage of questions fired at J. Bruce Ismay as he hurries out of the car with the door being opened for him in the mayhem of the arrival! Once again he is non-responsive to the demanding journalists and their questions, even if he was; he would not be able to answer them anyway because of the noise created by so many questions being asked by them!

One New York journalist stands in front of him, stopping him from going into the building.

'What the hell happened out there? Do they want you in first because they think you're responsible for this, Ismay? Where's the captain as well?'

Ismay stands there and looks at the journalist. This is the first time he is about to communicate with a journalist since the Carpathia docked in New York. There is a moment's silence.

'I honestly cannot properly explain what happened out there, to paraphrase the question. As far as being responsible for this disaster goes, I have to say you could never pinpoint such blame onto one person regarding the fact the Titanic struck an iceberg in the North Atlantic. You can take the discussion where you want as far as the entire thing goes as to what is right and wrong.' He continues. 'As far as representing the White Star Line on board Titanic, I honestly do not know what else to say, apart from the fact, can we remember all the passengers who unfortunately and tragically lost their lives in such a way at sea.' He pauses for a second and again continues. 'To answer your last question about the captain, I have no idea where he is. Now, if you don't mind, please get out of my way. I have this congressional investigation hearing to attend.' Replying in a recitation like way. Ismay and his wife walk up the steps into the building, where the investigations panel is waiting for him, with its detailed list of questions about what happened to Titanic.

They make their way inside the marbled floored building, and walk up the traditionally wooden spiralled staircase to the room where the hearing will be heard, where there is an intense atmosphere. The moment has arrived for J. Bruce Ismay to face his barrage of questioning as the panel are now waiting for him. When approaching the room, in the pine oaked decor of the building's interior, he is met by a representative who welcomes him to the hearing.

'Good morning Mr Ismay. Welcome to the congressional investigations here in New York. Can I now ask you to make your way alone into the room, where the congressional investigation panel are waiting to begin the official Titanic disaster inquests.'

'Very well, let's begin the hearing. I guess I have no choice but to take my place in this room and try to find the answers so badly needed at this moment.' Ismay responds, looking at the representative.

'Very well, Mr Ismay. Please enter. The congressional investigation is waiting.'

J. Bruce Ismay makes his way into the black and white, chess board style floor of the room, where the investigative eyes of the panel are looking at him as they have their questions ready for him concerning the Titanic. A reluctantly looking Ismay walks slowly to the centre of the room where his chair is waiting for him. One of the panel, who is seated in his chair central to his work colleagues, addresses the congressional hearing.

'Mr Ismay, please be seated.'

'Thank you.' Bruce Ismay replies, after a short pause, as he looks up at the head of the panel.

With an air of anticipation accompanied by an atmosphere of sadness concerning the proceedings, a male member of the hearing, seated to the left-hand side and parallel with the head of the panel, begins the initial proceedings by saying.

'Could you please confirm your name and the company you are here to represent concerning the Titanic disaster.'

'I am Mr J. Bruce Ismay, the chairman of White Star Line.'

'Very well. Thank you for attending Mr Ismay.' As the head investigator looks up at him curiously and speaks with a cautious tone of voice.' He continues to address the hearing as he officially begins the proceedings. 'Mr Bruce Ismay, you are called here before these congressional hearings as a representative of the White Star Line company. You are, without doubt, the head of the company's representation and in particular you are this person out at sea as well, taking full responsibility for the conduct of your chairmanship of this company. Do you agree with this Mr Ismay?'

'Well, I would guess so. That is generally the idea of the expected conduct in the representation of the company.' As J. Bruce Ismay responds, looking back at the head of the investigation with a slight look of exhaustion.

'Please do not use phrases too open, referring to the comment of 'I would guess so' as this does not imply a definite chairmanship and at the same time, makes one question your position as the White Star Line chairman when observing one's adequate psychology.' The head of the panel replies to Ismay

Ismay, now looking like he had seen every ghost and life of the Titanic, takes a sip of water from a small glass beside him, and in doing so; it looks like a drink of the water is very much required!

Another man to the right-hand side of the head investigator now begins his involvement in the congressional hearing.

'Mr Bruce Ismay, going off the evidence handed to us referring to wireless transmissions in the early hours of 15th April, 1912, there were distress signals sent from RMS Titanic in the form of mayday calls to ships who were in the oceanic vicinity. These read the ship had hit an iceberg and was sinking by the head in the North Atlantic. Our position now, here at this congressional hearing, is to establish why those mayday calls were sent relating to what actually happened before the ship hit an iceberg and just as important, what the causes of this dreadful disaster were.' Ismay is addressed. As this particular member of the hearing contributes his insight.

'Very well, I understand.' J. Bruce Ismay replies. As the congressional investigations are now under way in hopefully establishing what happened to RMS Titanic on this transatlantic maiden voyage.

-Chapter 3-

World War I, the Britannic and the Lusitania

With what many would regard as the inevitable resignation of J. Bruce Ismay from the White Star Line, even after fully cooperating at the congressional investigations and later being exonerated by a British inquiry into the maritime disaster, many would also describe it as one disaster of a time as the chairmen. Combined with this, there is a changing of the guard atmosphere in the air, not just at the White Star Line but throughout society as well, with the outbreak of World War I following not long after this. Fortunately for Ismay, the company offers him a supply role of, as and when required at the White Star Line offices he accepts, considering the void appeared as to who is going to employ him anyway after the facts established following the congressional hearings.

In 1914, the world experiences the outbreak of World War I and this changes the mentality of society in general regarding how the so-called class system is perceived. The continued obsession with class continues right into the twentieth century and to the time of the outbreak of World War I is immensely diminished considering the country's need to unite as one during this time. There is a feeling in the air of the country needing to work together in one spirit considering World War I has started. That segregation of society, for so long that had been present in Britain, has now all but evaporated from the forefront of society and there is an unusual unified psychology now present

Throughout Great Britain, there is an atmosphere of a United Kingdom coinciding with the ending of the passenger-liner generation having experienced its peak around the early twentieth century. For the first time there has also been a change of focus regarding the

Titanic disaster and just how bad the loss of life had been felt in the aftermath of the disaster. There is now a different light on things relating to how everything has previously been perceived. There is a moving on to a completely different time because of how World War I has unfortunately come to be on the Earth.

Bruce Ismay's new-found role of supply worker at the White Star Line offices is a far cry from his days as the company chairman. He has also been relocated to a new emerald coloured office in the building he thinks has not quite got the same vibe and demeanour as his previous office. However, this is just what his situation is now meant to be. To be honest, he has to regard himself lucky to be continuing his employment at the company regarding his track record concerning what happened in the North Atlantic on board Titanic. This role will see him involved in supporting the administration of White Star Line with far less involvement in public relations duties than before, if any at all.

Not long after the new regime has been put into place at the company, World War I has broken out and there is a completely different atmosphere around the workplace in general and throughout the country. The psychology of society has now changed to one that is at war with the Germans. Not surprisingly, Ismay is beyond the age range for compulsory conscription. Privately, he is now existing in some sort of penance with his new found role at the company. It is a penance that could not be avoided considering the disaster at sea for which he is deemed responsible. His situation regarding consciousness of responsibility is one you would imagine requires a certain amount of improvement concerning his now disastrous record.

As the new White Star Line set-up continues at the company headquarters, Bruce Ismay is seated adjacent to his desk with his feet crossed upon it, reading a newspaper, when he hears a knock on his office door. It is the Irish office lad who works there that informs various employees of any news needing relaying to them throughout the working day. Ismay responds to the knock and pleasantly says.

'Hello. Come in.'

The Irish office lad opens the door.

'Mr Ismay, it's the Ministry of Defence. They want to speak to you about the Britannic!' He informs him in an excited manner.

Ismay looking a bit confused as to why they want to speak to him, pauses for a moment.

'I don't know why they want to speak to me' he replies in a surprised manner.

'Mr Ismay, they want to turn it into a hospital ship!' The office lad continues to inform him.

Bruce Ismay now might as well be on another planet, wondering how on earth they would achieve this, holds his hand up where he nearly falls off his chair.

'Pass me the phone. Are you sure it's the Ministry of Defence?' He now responds in a disgruntled tone of voice.

As things progress during the phone call, J Bruce Ismay in some way begins to change the way he has always looked at his own life and the society lifestyle he lives, including his perception of passenger liners. For the first time in his life, he now looks at a passenger liner in a completely different way to how he has perceived them previously. He is so intrigued by the fact the White Star Line gives the go ahead for the Britannic to be transformed into a hospital ship, he decides to attend the docking of the ship at Southampton harbour, where this former passenger liner is getting ready to set sail and become part of World War I on a lovely summers day, with a light breeze blowing in off the ocean.

More importantly, there are a few thousand soldiers gathered there waiting to set sail to France, some making their way onto the ship along with those already on board, there is very much an historic atmosphere in the air. Now newly named HMHS Britannic, the ocean liner will become a saving grace for the many casualties the ship will save, provide a sanctuary for and become a home to.

Back at the White Star Line office, a new lease of life has dawned where J. Bruce Ismay now seems to have turned the corner and he looks like a man who has started his long journey of redemption from his own life experiences where at times, could not have gone more wrong if anybody had actually attempted to make them go any worse. As time moves on, there is this real consciousness present the country is at war. At the same time, the everyday lives of many people continue as normally as can be because they have to. The country needs to show world war resilience considering the number of soldiers fighting on the front line for Great Britain, in conjunction with all the service men and women involved in the war!

J. Bruce Ismay is working through his usual administration, with assistance from a much-needed pipe and tobacco. Things are looking up considering how bad things were for him and the White Star Line after the Titanic disaster. He has found some sort of comfort in his administration support role at the company as he hears a knock at the office door. It's the Irish office lad.

'Mr Ismay, are you there?' He asks

'Yes, of course I am. Come in.' Bruce Ismay replies. Considering his new found optimism after such disastrous life experiences, Ismay is now psychologically anticipating some good news and wondering what on earth the lad is going to say next.

'Mr Ismay. It's the Ministry of Defence. We've lost the Britannic!' The office lad eagerly informs him.'

'What do you mean, we've lost it? Has the government purchased it?' Ismay replies in a jovial manner, thinking the office lad has turned into a stand up comedian. After a short pause he hastily takes a smoke of his pipe.

'No, Mr Ismay. It's sank! The lad replies.

Ismay turns away and nearly chokes on his pipe in sheer disbelief, not being able to take into account what has just been said! He stands up and yells at the office lad in sheer anger.'

'Get out! You silly Irish fool!'

'It's the Germans!' The office lad tells him passionately, adamant on informing Ismay of what has happened!

'I said get out and close the door!' Ismay shouts, becoming more incensed by the second.

'Mr Ismay, I will not be spoken to like that! They want you on the next train to London!' He responds with an increased tone of voice. The office lad makes his stand as a White Star Line employee and does not close the door.

Now in despair with his head in his hands, Ismay turns and replies.

'I'm not even the dam bloody chairman anymore!'

'You're the contact they've still got Mr Ismay.' The office lad enthusiastically informs him.

After the chairman of the White Star Line eventually hears the news of what is going on in the office and abroad, he immediately initiates his control of what now takes place over the coming days. In doing so, he instantly informs the Ministry of Defence J. Bruce Ismay will not be attending the meeting in Westminster because of the simple fact he is no longer the chairman of the company. Even if he was, he would not be on the next train to London after hearing about the sinking of HMHS Britannic. He is quite clearly psychologically not fit to attend a meeting with the Ministry of Defence considering his sadness in hearing about the loss of the Britannic. What has happened could not be any worse. He now thinks he is partly responsible for two of the White Star Line passenger liners being on the bottom of the sea!

In the midst of the commotion of World War I, there is another very well-known passenger liner destined to be involved at the forefront of things when it comes to transatlantic crossings during this unusual time in human existence. This ship is one of Cunard's fleet, named the Lusitania. Already a very experienced transatlantic maritime great, the Lusitania continues to make transatlantic journeys even after the outbreak of the war. These dangerous voyages continue into the early years of the war, considering the warning from other ships and naval staff that German U-boats are patrolling the waters of the Atlantic.

However, there is an agreement passengers liners cannot be fired upon considering they are not military vessels. Passenger liners also have no way of defending themselves against an attack because they are quite clearly built for civilian travel across the oceans. During negotiations between various countries involved in the war, they come to the conclusion, it is unthinkable ships such as the Lusitania could possibly be fired at and, without doubt, they do not allow for any such attack as the agreement is written out and signed by all those countries involved. Every country concerned in the world war and their military forces are made aware of the situation regarding the non-firing at oceanic passenger liners, but unfortunately not long passes before the Lusitania tragically also takes its place on the sea bed, just like the Titanic and the Britannic have done.

Not surprisingly, it is a German commander on board a U-boat who is the perpetrator ending this agreement regarding the firing at passenger liners. In all the paths of disaster a ship can take, it is tragically the case for the Lusitania, just as it was for the Titanic and the Britannic, they too should meet their end this way when sailing on the ocean. The Lusitania almost avoided such a disaster like these other two great ships, but the captain's decision so late on to change the direction in which they were travelling disastrously led the ship within the vicinity of a German U-boat having a lunatic captain on board who decided to fire a torpedo at this great transatlantic liner.

-Chapter 4-

The Olympic Troop Ship

J. Bruce Ismay eventually departs the White Star Line as the official face of the company throughout the passenger liner industry; a departure one would say was long overdue considering the Titanic disaster and the no-man's land atmosphere having descended on the company after the tragic sinking of the great ship. Why Ismay continued to remain employed at the forefront of the company, in the first place as the chairman, is anybody's guess, even though his tenor in the role was undoubtedly at its end considering the circumstances. The company decided it was clearly better off without Ismay's services as the White Star Line are now attempting to take their transatlantic ocean liner business in a new direction, if this is ever possible after a rather disastrous decade to say the least.

Another enquiry has been made at the White Star Line office concerning one of their fleet. It is the Ministry of Defence again and this time they have an interest in the Olympic. With sister ship, the Britannic, having become a hospital ship during World War I, the Olympic has also been presented with a similar destiny regarding its involvement in the naval operations. The Ministry of Defence is enquiring to the White Star Line to see if it can also borrow the Olympic, as there is an urgent need for another ship on the scene as the implications of World War I are now in full swing throughout the country and the world itself. When the ministry uses the term borrow, they more or less mean in a politically correct manner, they are going to offer the White Star Line a certain amount of money and on the conclusion of the war, the company would be offered an opportunity to buy the ship back, providing it is still sea worthy and it has not been sank!

The Irish office lad, who had previously been working his way up the ranks at the White Star Line headquarters in Liverpool, has been appointed the temporary chairman of the company. One or two of the employees have looked twice at him sitting in the office, manning the company at such a young age compared with them. However, things are starting to pick up and the dreadful atmosphere surrounding the company is at least improving as time is going on. The lad has brought an uplifting and rejuvenating aura to the company with his new-found role of more responsibility at the helm of the White Star Line. He is hoping to take the company in a new direction considering what happened to the passengers of Titanic and the actual ship itself. His first idea is to change the colour of the Olympic so the passengers looking at and boarding the ship immediately have a different image of the voyage and therefore the company itself.

As the plans are being made on the new colour of the passenger liners in the fleet, with new decor ideas being thought of as well for the ships and their interior design, the Ministry of Defence has made a another move on the White Star Line to recruit the Olympic for services in the British Army and Navy. At the company headquarters, the stand-in chairman is briefing his new team on how they will progress their ideas for the new design of the ships into practice, considering they are travelling back and forth across the Atlantic Ocean as serving passenger liners.

As the staff briefing begins, there is a knock on the door of the meeting room where the new office lad, also from the Republic of Ireland, opens the door without anybody calling him in and says.

'Mr Chairman, The Ministry of Defence is on the phone. They want to speak to you about the Olympic.'

'What on earth do they want? Hopefully they don't want the Olympic as well.' The new chairman replies, now in a moment's shock and wondering what on earth is going on.

'I don't know Mr Chairman. Maybe you should speak to them because they want to speak to you immediately.' The new office lad responds, with a surprised tone of voice.

'Right. Thanks. Tell them I'm on my way.' As the stand in chairman is now experiencing his first test at the helm of White Star Line. He makes his way to the office close by where the phone is situated as he picks it up and announces.

'Hello, this is the chairman of the White Star Line speaking. How can I help you? I do believe this is the Ministry of Defence I am communicating with. Can you hear me?'

'Yes. It is the Ministry of Defence Mr Chairman, if this is how I address you. Do you have a name?' A male voice replies.

'Yes, of course I do. That is it. I am known to my work colleagues as this and now I am known to you, the Ministry of Defence, as Mr Chairman.'

'Very well, Mr Chairman, I'll be straight to the point considering our nation is at war at this present time. The thing is, we need the Olympic as well! As the representative from the government is now becoming slightly more aware with the tone of the phone call!

'Wait a minute. You have already got the Britannic! You cannot just keep decommissioning the passenger liners!' The chairman shouts at him, stopping the representative in his tracks. The chairman is not happy with the fact the government assumes it can just borrow another ship from the company.

'The plan is we turn RMS Olympic into a troop ship and transport British soldiers on it, starting with a fleet leaving from Southampton.' The government representative informs him, as he tries his best to reassure the chairman this is for the best.

The chairman again is not happy with how the representative from the government is assuming he can just take another ship from the White Star Line, considering the Titanic is now on the bottom of the Atlantic and officially out of commission as one of the company's passenger liners. With the Britannic now out of commission as a passenger liner as well, having been turned into a hospital ship by the government and now on another seabed, you can understand his concerns the company does seem to be running out of ships! The government now wants to deploy the Olympic as a troop ship immediately with the transporting of soldiers to various locations, having been made an immediate concern because of the war situation.

After the chairman has informed the Ministry of Defence he is going to phone them back in a moment as he considers how everything is going to be affected, he realises he honestly has no choice as far as the situation goes. He is employed by a company he has now genuinely recognised should not be solely focused on company profits, considering the country is at war on many fronts throughout the world. The time has arrived for the White Star Line to change its mindset in recognition of the reality now confronting the country. It looks like another ship is on its way to being deployed to the war. The Olympic is about to be commissioned as a troop ship. The chairman has now prepared what he is going to say to the Ministry of Defence. The phone is ringing and the call is underway. The chairman has made his decision about the destiny of the Olympic. He is now ready to address the government, not in the usual houses of parliament manner, but down a phone line to communicate his decision.

The phone is answered in Westminster as the south-eastern accent of the secretary for the Ministry of Defence welcomes the stand-in White Star Line chairman as she says politely.

'Good afternoon. The Ministry of Defence.' The chairman is now ready to address her government colleague with who he has previously liaised.

'This is the chairman calling from the White Star Line. Could you please put me through to the minister I have been liaising with concerning RMS Olympic.'

'Thank you for returning the call to the Ministry of Defence. You will now be connected to him.' The secretary replies.

'Hello, Member of Parliament speaking from the Ministry of Defence concerning the inquiry about RMS Olympic.' As the government official introduces himself.

'Through all the principles of a fair and honest consciousness, one would say another approach by the government to take, not borrow these ships, which are probably never going to be seen again by the White Star Line, is an extremely abrupt way of conducting one's self. Considering the magnitude of the Titanic disaster combined with the Britannic becoming a hospital ship and sinking. As a government representative you must now be aware to some extent you are without doubt, taking liberties regarding the attempted dispersal of the White Star Lines ocean liner fleet.' The Chairman communicates immediately, with a professional assertiveness regarding the situation.

Before the chairman continues addressing the government official, who is listening with an air of anticipation on the other end of the phone line in Westminster, the representative attempts to speak to him as he says.

'Well, with one's country now at war with Germany, you would expect.'

'No, please do not interrupt me, as I have not finished speaking to you yet. As I was implying to you about the concept of taking liberties regarding the White Star Lines' ocean liner fleet, this is without doubt how you have come across in your conduct to recruit the company's ships. As the chairman of the company, I now have to make it very clear to you we do not take kindly to the fleet ending up on the ocean floor and being de-commissioned by these German U-boats, whatever they are!' He continues. 'However, I also have to make it clear to you, as the chairman of the White Star Line; we take our position as a military asset in an extremely proud way as well. Therefore we see it as our duty to this country to now deploy RMS Olympic as a troop ship, to play a pivotal role in the hope Great Britain can be led to victory in this war with Germany.'

'Well, Mr Chairman, never in all my time working for the government and throughout my life in general itself, have I ever heard anything so inspirational with such an atmosphere of optimism and truly all-inspiring words as far as this country goes. I have to say I am delighted to hear the news the Olympic can now play such an important part in contributing towards the success of Great Britain in World War I. Hopefully we can now begin to turn the ship into an adequate military ship as soon as possible, as we need to change certain parts of it from civilian features into military focused areas.' The government official proudly replies after listening to such a great speech.

'Very well. The Olympic is now decommissioned as a passenger liner and is immediately re-commissioned in full military service, authorised by the White Star Line company as from today.'

-Chapter 5-

The End of an Era

The year is now 1916 and four years have passed since the Titanic disaster. One of the lifeboat commanders has found life very difficult since that fateful night in the North Atlantic. Back in Southampton, England, where he lives, this particular crew member who was in command of a particular lifeboat he was assigned to is in his home. There is a pleasant spring breeze and early summer air outside his house. After being tormented in his own thoughts about the lifeboats not returning, especially the one he was manning, as a last resort, he takes his own life: because the guilt of not returning and watching people dying has taken its toll. Out of all the lifeboats, only two returned to the scene where the Titanic disappeared into the sea. The psychological consequences have tragically impacted upon this man; he genuinely did not want to be alive anymore living with the guilt of rowing away from the sinking area with most of the other lifeboats during a life changing experience at sea night. . In addition to this, he was too old to be conscripted for World War I.

On the subject of conscription, the former Titanic watchtower officer, Charles Lightoller, has been assigned to work for the British army on board the former passenger liner RMS Oceanic. In the two years since the tragedy, Lightoller continued to be employed by the White Star Line in his regular officer duty role for the company's fleet. However, the time has now come for him to take military responsibility as a member of the British army, with the country having now gone to war with Germany.

'Lightoller,' a crew member calls, as the ship docks at the port of Gibraltar in the Mediterranean. 'Give me a hand with this door; we need to turn this wheel and get the gangway connected to the harbour.'

'Very well, I usually do that myself though. However, I understand we need to be prompt considering the large number of soldiers and military personnel who are about to depart the ship!' Lightoller replies enthusiastically.

This is a real change of scenery for people like Charles Lightoller; they have gone from the working routine of passenger liners to a complete change in psychology as to how they present themselves in uniform on board a ship. This change of working atmosphere is unusual in a way because the pre-World War I life seems like it never existed before in a strange paradox manner, because the world is now at war.

Another society is now present compared to a completely different one having previously existed which was defined on class and a social system, with its financial hierarchy. This segregated society has now had no choice but to become one with different classes coming together and fulfilling the aim of saving one's country from German rule in these challenging times of war for Great Britain!

On the other side of Europe Henry Morgans is on his way to the Somme in France as he has conscripted himself to the British army. After deciding his maritime involvement had come to an end regarding officiating himself on board any of the transformed passenger liners now being military ships. It is the beginning of a new era in his existence, along with the other World War I British army conscripts that are now also on their way to the Somme. A convoy of military personnel are making their way towards the Somme as the French country roads are directing the British contingent in the form of many army trucks to the place they are destined to go into battle with a dangerous Germany army. It is a glorious July summers day in the year of 1916 out in the French countryside as the British army are about to begin the battle of the Somme. The British soldiers are in great spirits as they are seated opposite one another other in their designated vehicles where they are about to arrive at the British trenches in France. The company comes to a halt as the convoy arrive at the correct location.

'Company. Halt!' Is the command faintly heard amongst the last few vehicles arriving at the trenches. A number of lieutenants immediately make their way to the rear of the soldier's vehicles having now stopped and unlock the back doors of them.

'Company, attention!' The lieutenant shouts. 'You will now depart your designated military vehicle and make your way to the side of the road where you are required to form an orderly line. In doing so, you are asked to wait patiently to be addressed. This is the point where you will be signed in by your general and will be officially registered as a British soldier at these trenches, here to fight in the battle of the Somme. Thank you for your co-operation and good luck.'

After only being there a few days the British soldiers are informed by those in command they are about to go into battle and make an attempt to advance over the battle ground in the Somme by beginning an attack on the German front line. Two other soldiers who are with Henry Morgans from their Titanic days are fellow survivors, R.N. Williams and George Rheims. These two men are known as true heroes of Titanic because of how they returned in collapsible lifeboat A to save as many people as they could. Only two boats returned to the sinking of Titanic in 1912 to save passengers who were stranded in the Atlantic Ocean. George Rheims saved a man from dying after he rescued him from the ocean and into the lifeboat. The man asked Rheims if he could give him a picture of himself with a dedication fit for the King of England!

The order is given by the commander. The British army on the front line are told to get ready for battle. The soldiers are about to make an advance on the German front line by crossing over no-man's-land.

'Wait for the whistle' the lieutenant orders. After a short pause the command is given 'Attack!' The lieutenant shouts from inside the trench as he blows the whistle almost immediately after shouting his order. The British soldiers quickly start to climb the wooden ladders of all the trenches and make their way out into the summer sun. A dash for no-man's-land begins as their assault on the German front line is under way in the heat of the day; the battle for the Somme in France has commenced!

Meanwhile, the reality of the consequences regarding the Titanic disaster having faced Francesca Draycott and her loved ones is they have survived in New York City without the luxuries and wealth they previously had in their lives for the time being. Francesca's fiancé, George Edwards, was reunited with her for not long after docking in New York City on board the Carpathia. For a few years, George lived the working-class lifestyle with Francesca where they had a wonderful time living a modest existence. However, upon the outbreak of World War I, George Edwards had to leave New York and return to England as a British soldier as military conscription was compulsory for all men registered as British Citizens.

Unfortunately, during the allied advance to victory, Francesca Draycott receives the dreaded news her fiancé and British soldier George Edwards has died in action after coming under fire from a German shell attack on the front line. This being so near to the end of the war during the Hundred Days Offensive in 1918 at the culmination of World War I.

For Francesca and her mother they continue working at various factories to make a living for they with both of them experiencing a complete paradox to their previous luxurious lifestyle, with her father Humphrey working at a casino and local bar. They are both kept alive by the fact they can drink at this bar a few times a week near to their apartment, where they have managed to gain a tenancy. They have been given a lease of life by the fact they can free their minds and consume alcohol at this entertaining place in New York as Francesca is overcoming the passing of her fiancé. Francesca seems to have an air of optimism about her and at times is finding her modest lifestyle and workplace rather enlightening compared what she and her mother were used to beforehand when they lived a more up market lifestyle. However, her mother is more suicidal, working in a cotton factory and not spending the money like she had previously, her reality has become everything she feared and worse, at worse she envisaged working in a high-class type of establishment, but lady luck has sent her to the hard working factories of New York City on short-term contracts. Her husband Humphrey has told her she will have to pull her weight regarding the income, because a substantial amount of his money is now on the bottom of the Atlantic after sinking with the Titanic.

For Vivienne, the thought of being an everyday worker once seemed more like the end of the world; to be honest it now seems more like the life of a monarch compared with where she has been working. She occasionally takes a walk and looks out at the Statue of Liberty. From time to time wondering whether or not she would be best sailing back past the thing in a passenger liner and returning to England with her husband and daughter. However, the thought of Francesca is keeping her going and therefore keeping her alive. Her duty as a mother is the defining thought as to why she has not bothered to suggest going back across the Atlantic, as the idea was, and is to stay in America for the time being.

Francesca's mother already has a craving for wealth again but she has a slight acceptance in herself she is still alive with Humphrey and Francesca, where she initially accepts the situation. However, this is replaced as time goes on with her becoming even more desperate of life in New York City in the situation in which she finds herself. She starts sending letters to acquaintances. She makes enquiries to old friends about other opportunities she thinks must somehow and somewhere be there for her. Thankfully, before she ends up calling it a day, she receives a reply from old business acquaintance, Molly Brown, about an opportunity to move to where she is and work with her.

This is where Vivienne and Francesca decide to move to Boston, Massachusetts for a new beginning in their lives. Mysteriously at the same time the entertaining piano player Humphrey Draycott and his upbeat orchestral group have been signed! With a tour of the United States planned, this conveniently coincides with the departure of his wife and daughter from New York City as a new era begins. He wishes them all the best in moving to Boston and plans to reside there as well when the tour is over.

The nine years Vivienne regards as the worst in her life, working and surviving in the big apple, actually seem more like nine hundred to her. Regardless, she has survived this life experience and has gradually come through a challenging test destiny had handed to her. The year of the move to Boston for Francesca and her mother is 1921. A new dream has arrived for Vivienne; she is now feeling some optimism, considering the opportunity Molly has handed to her in the face of inner turmoil regarding living and working where she was. The train leaving the station in New York, heading for Boston, Massachusetts, is an even more glorifying experience for Vivienne than the Titanic leaving Southampton!

As the train leaves New York City on a glorious summer's day, Vivienne hopes she is leaving her previous employment for the last time in her life. If she had planned out her life as she departed the Carpathia at New York harbour after surviving the sinking of the Titanic, she could not have wished for a more undesirable employment experience. Fate could not have dealt out a harder path for Vivienne if anyone had planned it out for her in the first place regarding working. It is quite strange she has not got the luck needed at times, because this state has always been associated with being somewhere you do eventually get a lucky break in your pursuit of glory. The paradox to this well-known experience is for the time being Vivienne was destined never to have immense wealth again in New York, as the mystery of all their lives continues.

They are now travelling to a new life where opportunity awaits them in Massachusetts, because of the lifeline an old business friend has thrown them in the form of the woman they call the unsinkable Molly Brown! She is currently the manageress of a well-known hotel within the vicinity of Boston's number one vacation resort! This is the place to visit in Massachusetts as far as the tourist industry goes in the state. Molly could see both Vivienne and Francesca working at her hotel amongst their friendly holiday atmosphere. This searching for a new opportunity has arrived at the perfect time for Vivienne as Molly Brown is even considering expanding the hotel and trying to become Boston's number one tourist attraction. Exciting times are ahead!

-Chapter 6-

The Move to Massachusetts

After what turned out to be a great escape for Francesca's mother Vivienne from New York City, they have now both arrived in Boston where Vivienne's great friend Mrs Margaret Brown, is waiting to meet them upon arriving at the station as they are about to depart the train. The journey from New York has been a liberating one for both women considering at times they were working twelve-hour shifts on short-term contracts at various locations throughout New York City. With the year's having now passed since the Titanic disaster and the way Francesca and her parents had to settle down to their challenging new lifestyle, those years were more like one hundred for Vivienne. Things are looking up for her and she now seems to have this certain strength in her, to the point where she will not again consider sailing back across the Atlantic Ocean and returning to England.

The train stops with a high-pitched breaking sound and comes to a complete halt, where there is a platform officer waiting to open the door of the wooden oaked coloured interior of the carriage Francesca and Vivienne are waiting to depart. They both depart the carriage as the sun shines on their face where they step of the train as the platform officer welcomes them and the rest of the party to the train station in saying.

'Welcome to Boston, Massachusetts everybody, your journey is complete!

Molly Brown, as always, is full of life and optimism when meeting Vivienne and Francesca at the train station, where straight away she notices the past few years have quite clearly taken it out of them both. As she approaches them, there is an immensely subdued atmosphere coming from both travellers from New York. Molly greats them with a warm welcome.

'Hello! Great to see you both my friends. Welcome to Boston, Massachusetts.'

Vivienne and Francesca, now with almost nothing left financially apart from the renewed optimism the move to Massachusetts has given them, both look at Molly where Vivienne says in an appreciating way.

'Thank you' and they hug one another in what is a really nice moment, considering it has been quite a few years.'

Molly then turns to Francesca, who says politely.

'Molly, how nice to see you.' They also embrace one another with a loving hug in a moment's reunion.

As they are making their way towards the eighteenth century church like exit of the train station, Molly informs both Vivienne and Francesca how she came to open the Boston hotel that she has managed for quite some time. Upon informing them of the gradual process of how she first took an interest in the hotel business, it is Vivienne who first shows an enthusiastic interest in working there and asks how she could also progress through the hotel employment spectrum.

'Sounds wonderful Molly, I think I could be very successful here in working for the hotel and gradually working my way towards the management employment opportunities with the hotel.'

'Sure Vivienne, I can sense you have that longevity required to one day go onto management of some kind but first of all my advice would be to just get used to how the hotel works and become familiar with the various roles of employment the hotel provides.' Molly informs her.

At times throughout her life, Molly could see herself in this line of business after experiencing many enjoyable stays as a hotel resident throughout her life to date, but for such a long time she stayed within the oil trade. Here she still has business contacts as this was the industry where Molly Brown was educated as a business woman.

As Molly and Vivienne are really enjoying discussing the possibilities of the hotel and what opportunities there could be, Francesca looks as though she is in a world of her own. She appears to have no interest whatsoever in the discussion of possible employment at the hotel. Either that or she is just listening and in a bit of a daydream. At this point Molly looks over and calls to Francesca.

'Francesca my dear, are you there?' Francesca does not reply having not appeared to have heard her. Molly calls over to her again saying, 'Francesca, you look miles away. Are you all right?'

Francesca finally comes out of her day dream and replies

'Sorry, I was on my own planet then listening to the train leaving, having flashbacks of the past few years of all that has happened in my life.' As they all now make their way towards the circular taxi rank area looking forward to hopefully a rather peaceful journey.

When arriving at the hotel the taxi driver reminisces. As the vehicle approaches the beige concrete flagged arrival area, driving slowly, he comments.

'When I drive in here, it always reminds me of a golf club I used to play at. You know this driveway for the car. This place has a bit of a racecourse aura to it as well.'

'Nice to hear, a lot of my family members play golf; some have their own racehorses as well. It's funny you've said that.' Molly replies.

'I wouldn't mind playing the game again myself to be honest, but I doubt I'll ever own a racehorse thinking about it. I'm someone who is supposed to have a bet on the horses now and again and hopefully have a few winners from time to time!' The driver says.

Molly laughs and replies.

'I know what you mean; personally I think the money goes out of the window at them races when you genuinely want your name on the trophy, I think it's a similar experience though as betting on the winner!' The car pulls up outside the main hotel entrance where the taxi driver opens the cab door from the driver's seat. He then gets out and helps unload the luggage.

After this, Molly asks.

'How much do I owe you?'

'That's three dollars please madam.' The driver replies. After exchanging the money for the journey, the taxi drives away and gives them a beep of the horn, showing a good spirited departure with an outgoing and friendly atmosphere.

When walking through the hotel entrance area, immediately there is a buzz about the place both Francesca and Vivienne sense as they approach the elegant black and white marbled floor reception area. Francesca now seems to be uplifted by the hotel's atmosphere.

'The place has a bit of New York about it with a countryside atmosphere as well.' She says optimistically.

Molly introduces them to one of the hotel's receptionists, whose shift it is when they arrive. The afro-Caribbean man welcomes them to Boston, Massachusetts where he says in a strong Jamaican accent.

'Welcome to the Glory. Good to see you both here.' They are both delighted with how the gentleman welcomes them and straight away feel at home as an oil lamp shines above at the back of the reception desk. For the first time since the Titanic disaster, there is an uplifting hope in the air they have not experienced since the day they both boarded the Titanic in Southampton.

Molly is called to a staff briefing where she is scheduled to address the hotel's employees on various staff procedures for the forthcoming shifts and events being held at the hotel. She is in jubilant mood and says to Vivienne, who is standing beside Francesca.

'No time like the present girls, you can come and join the fun!' They all make their way to the briefing area in the hotel's spacious main hall room where there is a nice summers breeze blowing through the hotel. Here Molly invites her newly arrived friends to take a seat and become even more familiar with the hotel's employment vibe at the Glory. Vivienne and Francesca have ultimately moved to Massachusetts to be engaged in this employment arena. Francesca takes a seat with her mother in the navy blue decor of the room, including the seats themselves although silver framed and comfortably cushioned.

There is an air of optimism from everyone at the hotel, where they can sense hope for the future as the team briefing is about to begin. Francesca and her mother have survived well in New York City so they should be thrilled to be in Massachusetts because, as far as employment is concerned, they have moved to a better place. They now have the chance to work with Molly Brown at the Glory where a new era is beginning!

Molly starts the briefing by thanking everyone for their recent efforts in delivering excellent customer service and maintaining a high standard at the hotel. She begins.

'Please be seated and settle down everyone. This afternoon I would like to truly thank you for your recent efforts at the hotel. We have continued to achieve a high standard of customer service here at the Glory while at the same time ensuring a continuing jubilant aura in the working atmosphere.' This standard is what Molly Brown inspires as the manageress and the ultimate standard she expects from her workforce at the Glory hotel. At the end of her speech, the hotel workers applaud her in the manner and culture of the hotel and the atmosphere generated by Mrs Margaret Brown.

Francesca and Vivienne have just taken part in their first official staff meeting at the Glory in Boston, Massachusetts. However, as Molly looks over to them both, they are both unusually quiet considering they have just arrived at a place of new beginnings as well as just becoming part of the hotel staff. Francesca looks more as though she has just been sentenced to death at the local courtroom with immediate effect. Vivienne looks even worse. She, for some reason resembles someone who has just been sentenced to death via death row, with both of them having a comical and subtle presence at the same time. Molly makes her way over to them both as she says in a jubilant manner.

'What did you think of that girls? Great atmosphere about the place isn't there?'

'That was quite an inspirational speech Molly; I like how you inspire the hotel workers as they are listening to you.'

'Francesca how lovely of you to say that, I can sense the Titanic survivor, now this is your new place full of so much hope, be that upbeat girl I always came to know?'

'Well, we have to stay strong Molly, I think I'll be alright, we have just experienced a long journey from New York. I like the person you perceive me to be, it must be those factories in New York City.' She says in an amusing and inspiring manner. Francesca continues. 'There's a great future for us here Molly, I just think I need a good night's sleep now.'

'Come over here and let me give you a big hug girl' where she stands up and embraces Molly Brown as they both share a loving embrace with one another. Molly then turns to Vivienne as she says. 'Vivienne, you come over here as well. Let me give you a big hug, great times are here for you as well girl. You look like you've been freed from having the weight of the world put on your shoulders there Vivienne.'

-Chapter 7-

The Meeting of Ruben Edwards, John Albert and Francesca Draycott

On a spring evening towards the end of March in 1922, the people of this particular part of Boston, Massachusetts, are assembling on the area's main venue with an aura of great excitement in the air. This triumphant atmosphere is combined with a continued euphoria of winning World War I in November, 1918, as the victorious American soldiers have returned and are enjoying civilian life again. It is the place where working men and women of the area find another lease of life. It is a place that allows dreams to come to life and exist. The poets are gathering to share their writing which can take the listeners to another place; the musicians are set and ready to play to their listening community, the billiards room is ready for a night of determined competition at the green cloth coloured table, the darts room is also ready for some skilled games, the cards room is ready, the decks are stacked on the red and blue clothed tables set for tonight's eagerly awaited monthly entertainment!

The place is the bar the Wagon and Stagecoach, on one of the nights at this well renowned Boston bar for poets, along with the entertaining musicians booked to play there. The night progresses. A man named Ruben is shortly to be going on stage to read one of his poems. Others have been on throughout the evening and there is a classical band playing generating an enjoyable party atmosphere with dancing in full swing! This is the point leading up to Ruben Edwards experiencing an unusual lifetime's meeting where at the same time a man named John Albert and Francesca Draycott are more or less making their way towards one another's attention. However, before this, Ruben Edwards meets Francesca. They turn to each other as they are both in merry mood and enjoying a wonderful time after having a few drinks. This historic moment is one of comedy as Francesca says in a light-hearted way.

'George Edwards, you've come back to life, or is this somebody else?'

'Well no. I'm Ruben. Pleased to meet you. Ruben responds surprised and not having a clue what she's talking about. As Francesca erupts into laughter, holding onto her friend who she happens to be out with. Smiling, Ruben says.

'Was it something I said?'

As Francesca continues to be in a fit of laughter, Ruben is called on stage directly after meeting her where the home crowd are waiting to hear him. Ruben starts to read his poem, 'Night of a Lifetime.'

'Night of a Lifetime'

As we live this life, we live these memories that are you and me.
There'll be times you know, when there are more things to see.
I'll bring a thought, that is just for now,
Times I wonder, whether or not to take a bow.

So live your way, in a right way.
Generations will say, there's a better day.
So live your time, let it all shine,
Do you ever find the night of a lifetime?

Wherever a dream may go, there is still something inside too.
Whenever this is needed, that glow that stays alight in you.
Now and again you'll sing, and fly away,
Look to horizons, from the bay.

> *So live your way, in a right way.*
> *Generations will say, there's a better day.*
> *So live your time, let it all shine,*
> *Do we ever find the night of a lifetime?*

Just before the crowd applauds, Francesca says something to finish it off after Ruben has completed a mesmerising performance. His poem's last line is 'Do we ever find the night of a lifetime?'

'Maybe some nights we do.' Francesca replies from the crowd.' At this moment, the crowd cheers and the rapture is great! Following this there is a glorious moment in time occurs when Francesca meets John Albert for the first time!

He looks into her eyes as he says.

'Maybe we just did' in the euphoria of the crowd's applause! Mysteriously Francesca's heart and soul appear to be cured at the same time here.

Following on from this initial meeting, all three of them are all set to get to know one another, as well as other individuals in their lives, after this memorable night, in the following days and weeks with a touch of déjà vu in the air. Ruben seems to have a presence of curing Francesca's bereavement of George Edwards, her fiancé who died in action so near to the end of World War I during the allied advance to victory in 1918. At the same time, she has started to experience similar chemistry with another romantic connection in the form of a man named John Albert in another time and place.

However, initially there's a pause to things, Francesca tells Ruben he has a brother or twin brother, but does not know which of the two it is. Ruben is completely unaware he even had a sibling as he is informed. Francesca is slightly bemused at first, thinking how does this lad actually exist. In the midst of all this she is getting caught up in another love at first sight, intense romance and actually wondering what on earth is going on!

As time progresses, John Albert and Francesca eventually fall in love with one another. Francesca naturally gets used to the circumstances surrounding the situation in the way she has met Ruben Edwards as well. Ruben is a miner by day in Boston and a poet by night, living a double existence so to speak. John Albert has a similar existence. He is also working as a miner by day for the moment, as well as being known locally as an actor by night. Francesca is employed in the souvenir shop at a local hotel, where she has actually found some sort of sanctuary from her life experiences to date. Just like in New York City her employment has continued her independence from any spoilt child atmosphere possibly present, along with her mother's sergeant major orders! She has mysteriously found a similar double existence in this part of the world with one of her truly loved passions, her own novel writing.

Ruben is engaged in his double existence as a poet and a miner for the time being. In his adventure through life, he earns the core of his money working in the local mines of this part of his hometown in Boston. This work is challenging physically compared to the thinker's train of thought when he is in a realm of creativity as a poet. It is not a challenge in the sense he does not like the physical exertion involved but his attitude works well and brings out his determination as a miner when working a shift down the mines with his fellow workers. This one realm to the next mindset in his life works well for him where he experiences the best of both worlds because he loves his poetry but asserts just as much effort into working as a miner as well.

The team atmosphere is a defining one for the miners in their daily quest to succeed. There is a determined resilience to their dynamic as a working team which includes comedy even subtle at times. Generally, they have a good understanding of one another as they have to working unison when carrying out a successful shift in these challenging mines. They say the most successful teams have an element of variety in the different individuals present in the team and things are no different here. In fact, these miners are on the same wavelength.

As time goes on, there is a sense it is time to move on from where they are in their lives. There is an atmosphere of new beginnings somewhere else. It appears Ruben has conquered himself and the area he lives in, not in a way that is bad and he thinks he is better than everyone, just to the point where his work, his poetry, should be heard in other parts, at other venues as well. He is really loved as a poet. He has proved his point about himself, to himself, to the point he is not only alive to be a miner. As much as he is a fundamental part of the miners' workforce and who they are within the community, he is also creative in his mind, where part of his mind, heart and soul are with his love of being a poet.

Francesca is also becoming partial to a move somewhere else, seeing as though her mother is up to her old tricks again, acting like a sergeant major. Vivienne is now employed as manageress of the hotel's restaurant. She is not only possessed to the point where she is ordering her daughter not to jump head first into another disaster of a relationship, she is telling her to forget about her art work. Vivienne wants Francesca to concentrate on her hotel career and, just as she has, put all her psychological energy into her career at the hotel's souvenir shop.

It is around this time John and Francesca are set to depart from Boston because with everything that is going on things seem to be culminating towards them moving away from where they are in their lives. They say there comes a time when you just know it's time to move on and this happens to be theirs. They decide it is now time for them as they move to New York to escape; the city is a well renowned place for making a living out of poetry as well as acting. Maybe this is the place where Ruben Edwards can find a second home on his creative quest, if not his first! The year of this move to New York City is 1922.

Moving to New York coincides well with the post-World War I epoch as people are experiencing this crest of a wave atmosphere as America and its allies have won the war. The end of the war has brought a sense of new hope to the country in the midst of what has been a time of so much uncertainty. For Ruben, his fiancée Anna, John Albert and Francesca Draycott this has to be the time in their lives when they seize the day and make the most of the atmosphere regarding new beginnings descended on the country. John Albert and long-time friend Ruben Edwards are two of those American soldiers who have luckily returned from serving their country. In no way is this new era detrimental to the memory of the soldiers having lost their lives for the liberty of the people of their country. These people died for the future of their country during World War I. Now opportunity awaits for those who have the chance to fulfil their dreams in this new age.

New York awaits these four charismatic individuals. There is a sense of a new life in this part of America for the talents these four bring with them after learning their trades in Boston. The acting opportunities of Broadway are waiting for John Albert as he is about to step into new auditoriums as an up and coming actor in this new state he is hoping to make his home. His experience will hold in him in good stead for the chances destined to come his way as he perseveres with his dreams as an actor. This is the ultimate ambition he has always thought he could achieve one day in the pursuit of his quest in acting. As for Ruben Edwards as well, he now has the same lifetime's opportunity to go and achieve his dreams on Broadway in New York City as an up and coming poet. He will, without doubt, have the poetic opportunity to thrive as an individual on his personal quest poetically. Just like as he and his good friend John Albert have worked as miners in the same team during their lives in

Massachusetts, they can now shine together on their creative pursuits, again in the same part of the world!

-Chapter 8-

Moving back to New York

As the lives of these four extravagant individuals progress to New York City, they arrive in the hustle and bustle of a busier place. They are now in a city with a more intense cultural atmosphere. However, this change of place in their lives does not faze them. They all truly take to this part of the world as naturally as possible and are engaged immediately in the razzmatazz of the city. It is well known you either take to New York City and these types of places or you don't. What happens with these four adventurers is the first scenario; they are all at home here in their new residency more or less straight away on their arrival from Boston. They also have an air of optimism quite inspiring and a force to be reckoned with!

As the train arrives in New York, the four hopefuls have experienced what they think is a life-changing journey because of the opportunities awaiting them in this dream-fulfilling state. Ruben Edwards and John Albert can hear the entertainment district of Broadway, Manhattan, calling them to the main auditoriums of this really special place. They now hope their destiny is there for them, these are exciting times as Ruben, Anna, John and Francesca all arrive in New York in this euphoric atmosphere. The train comes to a halt where there is a platform officer waiting to open the door of the carriage that all four of them are waiting to depart!

It is the poet from Boston, Massachusetts, Ruben Edwards, that is ready and waiting to depart the carriage first as he looks up and steps off the train. The platform officer welcomes him and the rest of the party saying.

'Welcome to New York City everybody, your journey is now complete!'

'Thank you very much. It is truly great to have arrived here in this great place.' Ruben replies enthusiastically. John Albert follows next as he now makes his way off the carriage as Francesca and Anna are next in the queue of people who are departing the train. At this point John Albert slips on the bottom rung of the train steps and almost takes everybody else with him on leaving the train, in what is almost an absolute farce of an incident in what should be something so normal!

Ruben and Anna immediately help him up with Francesca as it looks like assistance is very much required as John Albert comments rather comically.

'I think I'm getting on a bit! If not there was something in the tea, on this train we've travelled down here on, now please don't make me look an absolute imbecile, I could have got back up on my own!' As the other passengers are now looking on in a rather surprised way.

They settle into life in this historic city in the United States of America, Ruben starts to find out about the various bars and entertainment venues where they have poets speaking to the crowds; the places where people have assembled to listen to their creative works. This is a gradual process of finding his feet in this new city. Considering Ruben is already very much experienced in speaking to the crowds when reading his poetry to the eagerly awaiting audiences, he makes good progress in creating an awareness of himself as a poet in New York. The experience of being a well-known poet in Boston holds him in good stead to do well in this new found place. The adventure has started for this poet; Ruben Edwards has arrived in New York City to continue his creative quest!

On one particular evening, Ruben has made his way to the centre of Manhattan looking for other entertainment venues where he can continue to spread the word, so to speak, in his pursuit of poetic glory, just like in the same way he has already achieved in his birthplace of Boston. The bar he sees in the distance is a place called the Valentine Inn. Inquisitive as to whether or not it is a poet-speaking type of place. Ruben makes his way over there and walks in. He is greeted by what sounds like someone with a German accent speaking to the audience; Ruben can sense an air of opposition straight away. Is there an early rivalry in the air with these two poets now encountering one another? After the German finishes his poem, the host addresses the crowd and announces,

'Ladies and Gentlemen! Please put your hands together … for Lars Winserheinen!' Ruben naturally applauds just like everyone else. He truly appreciates fellow poets and, at the same time, he now knows who this German is. He has become aware of Lars Winserheinen!

Over the coming weeks, Ruben makes a few appearances at the Valentine Inn, reading to the audiences his work that they have never heard before. He also reads new poetry to them that he has recently written upon living in New York. The reception he receives is the same as it was in Boston; the audiences of New York know that he has something about him as a writer and poet as he is inspiring the imagination of the crowds with his creativity! Ruben really takes to New York, not just as his residency, but also to the stages just as much, similar to how he did back home in Boston, Massachusetts. He is also writing his poetry with a different concept considering his life experiences in New York City. On the occasions Ruben Edwards is reading his work to the audiences there is one man paying particular attention to him more than anyone else and this is fellow poet Lars Winserheinen. He is very apprehensive about him because he knows privately they are progressing to become immense rivals!

At first they are both more or less telling themselves to focus on their own work and not get caught up in a rivalry that could take command of the poetic atmosphere they both genuinely have. However, as the rivalry becomes visible, in the sense the audiences are becoming aware of it; there is a slight clash of personalities in the air as they are both privately aiming to be number one in New York City. The rivalry is clearly becoming an exciting one for everyone concerned, not only on the poetry scene but the competition is starting to capture the imagination right across the entertainment scene as well. Throughout New York you can really sense the build up to poetry slam!

There is also another poet who has caught the imagination of the New York audiences having been given his stage name by the New York crowds just like some of the other poets; this entertainer is Irishman Terry King from the Republic of Ireland, who also comes from Manchester, England as well. On the creative scene in New York they are staring to call him The Ruler as he entertains on stage!

With poetry slam fast approaching in the middle of a cool New York summer, there are many poets who are eagerly awaiting the contest, and at the same time, fancy their chances of claiming the award. In doing so, they would be the one conquering New York as a poet. There are a few international poets that could win this and Terry Ruler is not the only Irish poet who has a chance of being a triumph and winning. There are a number of American poets who also fancy their chances amongst the contenders to be potential winners of poetry slam. There are also a number of Canadian poets having also travelled to New York seeking their destiny as poets. As far as this contest goes, poetry slam can take you to another place in your poetic existence when it comes to making a breakthrough. However, the winner of this contest is no foregone conclusion. It is genuinely anybody's to win!

Ruben and Anna are starting to do well for themselves in New York City and are really enjoying life with Ruben now hoping to be the winner of poetry slam. This is the most well-known competition for poets in New York and the competition is even covered by the *New York Times*. The winner can make it into the local newspapers with their poetry success!

Ruben is also planning to earn his living from his poetry, which has always been his dream. Francesca Draycott finds another passion in her life as well working as a photographer. Their lives have now taken a course handing them an eventful destiny in more ways than one. Things start to get even more eventful for them both concerning the various individuals they begin to encounter.

With certain individuals now in New York City taking care of their affairs, there is more awareness starting to take place about who is who in this extravagant part of America. Things like this you could say take care of them self naturally as far as the social scene goes on Broadway in Manhattan but you could say this is not always for the better. With Ruben Edwards interviewed by the New York press along with other poets as well, himself Anna and Francesca have become quite familiar with the general public of this part of the world, the reason being Francesca has been photographed with Ruben and Anna. She has also been taking part in some interviews with Ruben when he has spoken with journalists. Not to the point where she is trying to take over the interview but with an inspirational presence as one of his friends. She has also become his photographer as well amongst the frenzy of the other photographers. Things are really starting to take off for everyone in New York with their careers.

You could say, with his fiancée, Ruben is now on his way to experiencing hedonism and sheer pandemonium considering he might become the reigning champion of poetry slam. They are extremely modest as they really take everything in their stride considering the continuing success of their adventure in New York to date. Within this time of their lives, of course, there is the personal experience of enjoying the whole thing in the sense they have created a lot of social awareness with coverage of pre-poetry slam in the New York press. John Albert and Francesca Draycott also seem to be enjoying this crest-of-a-wave atmosphere generated by the build up to New York's eagerly anticipated poetry slam contest. In a way,

Ruben has paved the way for John Albert to achieve something of himself as an actor when it comes to his own career. In his own way, John is experiencing the winning vibe currently present throughout the entertainment district of Broadway, Manhattan. It is therefore a perfect time for him to make something of himself as an actor in New York, as he, too, should go from strength to strength in achieving great things as his own dream is starting to become a reality.

There are many other people in New York City these four are surprisingly destined to encounter as well. Some of them are the last individuals on the planet they could do with running into considering their success to date in their new found home. It is the emergence of these individuals making way for some very eventful incidents as their adventure in New York is about to get into full swing. There are going to be some very exciting times, not just for Ruben Edwards with fiancée Anna but John Albert, with his other half, Francesca Draycott, are also destined to truly experience everything New York has to offer when it comes to realising their dreams!

-Chapter 9-

Poets of New York

A real creative euphoria has now arrived and is present throughout the poet scene in New York City with this atmosphere not just being experienced at the venues throughout Broadway. This vibe is starting to be sensed at various venues in other parts of New York as well. Many creative's are travelling to different parts of the city to establish themselves on this inspirational scene. This influx of poets from different parts of America has combined with the arrival of many from all around the world as well. New York City has become the place to be with the entertainment district of Broadway, Manhattan contributing in a truly charismatic like way to attracting so many talented people to the area. The state has become the place to be to fulfil one's dream in this line of creative performance.

Lars Winserheinen is full of hope in contesting for poetry slam this year. He has previously competed for the title upon being tantalising close to securing the trophy and being crowned the champion of poets. At the previous contest, Winserheinen ended up missing out on third place, in what was a dramatic end to poetry slam culminating in a classic atmosphere. He finished in fourth place to his amazement, considering he was being tipped to win the contest having previously reached two finals. Losing out on the final was a bad enough experience in itself, but to not secure the third place award was a devastating moment for the German, knowing how close he has come in the past to being crowned champion!

That night on the final evening of poetry slam in 1923 a poet from the West Indies, going by the name of Frankie Fortune, defeated Lars Winserheinen in a classic semi-final encounter on the final evening of poetry slam. Frankie Fortune went on to win the title on this occasion against Terry Ruler from the Republic of Ireland. The Irish-born poet came tantalisingly close to winning poetry slam but on this night he was crowned with his nickname as he walked up onto the stage to collect his finalist award. The crowd that evening started to chant 'Ruler, Ruler, Ruler, Ruler!' His nickname and stage name with the crowd was born. Even though he was not to be crowned champion some people were starting to call him the Ruler! Frankie Fortune won the crowd over by the narrowest of margins on this particular evening with his passionate approach and his poetry just gave him the vote from the judges as well. As close as the contest was he fully deserved his victory in New York City.

There is another poet who is making headway towards creating a name for himself in New York with his own words of inspiration. This poet comes from the Deep South! Tony Kingdom is his name and he is from the state of Mississippi in the USA. This guy knows how to word his poetry to the point where he shares his life experiences in a positive light but he lets you know it has been no bed of roses for him at the same time in the life he has lived so far. He inspires the crowds to the point where they understand this realism of what he is talking to them about because the majority of these people listening can relate to him. They appreciate what the man is talking about and saying to them as well. Tony Kingdom has a real-life approach, not only as a writer and poet but also as a person. He comes across to the audiences he speaks to in the way he tells them how he has made his way northwards on his creative journey from the state of Mississippi.

There is so much poetic talent in New York City even people like Tony Kingdom have challenges in winning contests like poetry slam because of the strong competition. At the same time the next poet knows they have to be something pretty special to be regarded as someone who is better than the likes of Tony Kingdom on their quest for glory!

There is also another personal rivalry breaking out on the poet scene, especially in the entertainment district of Broadway in mid-town Manhattan. Terry King seems to have now met some camaraderie competition in the form of Tony Kingdom. He appears to be the American version of a people-friendly poet and vice versa in the way Terry King is an Irish version, with this creative and social connection aura. At venues throughout this part of New York the audiences have given this Irishman his stage name. To make the atmosphere even more exciting, there are people in the crowds at these poetic venues now starting to call Tony Kingdom the 'King' as he walks on and off stage when addressing the audiences in New York City. The Ruler from the Republic of Ireland has found a rivalry with the King from Mississippi in a socially positive way for everyone concerned. They both continue to have this adulation from the crowds in an equal manner because these audiences know they are both great in their own ways! On one occasion at the poets' evening, just before Terry Ruler began speaking, an Irish comedian in the crowd shouted.

'Does he know Terry Pencil?' Where the crowd then erupted into euphoric laughter!

As far as poets of New York go, there is definitely one name you would not associate with creativity and poetry in all the galactic realms of the universe! This name is Bruce Ismay! But not the one the crowds think it is, in every sense of the name. This Bruce Ismay, the poet from Vancouver, Canada, is absolutely nothing like the one he shares his name with and in that sense; he might as well be from another planet. This man is a lot more thoughtful in his approach to life; he sees the good in as many hopeless situations as he can wherever he goes in his life. Whereas a certain other J. Bruce Ismay the majority of the time is a walking disaster when it comes to having any hope at all in people who appear not to be as fortunate as him in their human existence. He has the same name as this charismatic poet from Vancouver, but this is where they officially part company, because everything inspirational about this Canadian-born poet is everything that makes the other J. Bruce Ismay desolate and unfulfilled concerning his outlook on people and things.

Ismay the poet, has an historic connection with the audiences who he speaks to. You can picture the countryside of the different parts of Canada he refers to when he addresses the audiences. When he is speaking about the place he is from in Vancouver, you see a mountainous and picturesque place. The thing with this Bruce Ismay is he takes the listeners in the crowd to another place and the true talent in his words is where he honestly invites the listener to maybe visit these places he is talking about in his poetry. This poet has a natural realm to himself in the way he connects with the crowds. He definitely has his own stage presence, just as much as any other poet on the scene in New York enjoyed by the audiences throughout the entertainment district of Broadway, at the heart of the venues for poets in Manhattan.

The night has arrived. The venue is the Valentine Inn Broadway, Manhattan. Poetry slam is here and New York is about to see a winner collect the award and enjoy immense glory. Someone is about to be crowned New York's best poet! The way the contest works is the panel of judges vote for the poet they think is the best and the four who have been selected the most times go into a semi-final draw with a third place play-off and ultimately a final following this to determine who wins poetry slam! Where Ruben is from in Boston, there was always an inspirational atmosphere at the Wagon and Stagecoach, but this place takes the euphoria to another level considering there are so many people there from all over the world. The Valentine is the arena for creativity in New York City!

Poetry slam is in full flow! The way Ruben Edwards handles the pressure of the occasion and takes it all in his stride is magnificent. His performance is immense and there are a few outstanding performances from some of the other poets. Now the moment arrives for the host from Scotland to announce the finalists. He first says.

'Ladies and gentleman, please put your hands together for the first finalist tonight … Mr Lars Winserheinen! This is his third final!'

Then with sheer tension in the air and Ruben Edwards not even knowing if he has made the last four, the announcer informs the audience.

'Ladies and gentleman, please applaud the man who will also compete in this year's final with a chance to win … Mr Ruben Edwards!'

The relief is immense as Ruben and Anna share a loving moment as the crowd applaud the finalists! However before this, the third-place play-off takes place with just as much drama as could be, with Tony Kingdom of Mississippi in the USA defeating last year's champion Frankie Fortune from the West Indies! There is now one more encounter to decide the winner! With the last two poets now ready for the 1924 final!

With poetry slam tradition before the final the national anthems of the two finalists are played, this year's being the national anthems of Germany and the United States of America. They are about to be played by the orchestra who are ready and waiting on stage. The first is the German national anthem as Lars Winserheinen stands to attention with his entourage where they enjoy a proud moment listening and singing along to their national anthem. After this Ruben Edwards shares his moment as many of the audience assembled in the Valentine Inn sing along with him as well for the American national anthem, turning one or two of the German's heads because of how loud they are with so many of them singing! The first performance is by Lars Winserheinen, the last performance will be with Ruben Edwards!

The moment is here at last as the announcer from Scotland dramatically informs the crowd.

'The 1924 poetry slam champion is … Mr … Ruben … Edwards!'

The way Ruben Edwards handles the pressure of the occasion and takes it all in his stride is magnificent; his performance is legendary. After this, the atmosphere and celebrating is definitely the night of a lifetime as Ruben is awarded the trophy where he gloriously lifts it in the air! Lars Winserheinen's experience nearly beats him but the judges decide by one Ruben has done just enough to be crowned champion!

He is the agreed winner of New York City's poetry slam and wins the title of New York's best poet! To make the celebrations even better, the orchestra are about to perform a new song titled 'Nessun Dorma.' This has been written recently by composer Giacomo Puccini from Italy. The musical performance was arranged with the poetry slam organisers as the composer had been visiting New York and has contacts with the orchestra. The performance is one powerful display as well as being musically captivating with everyone in the audience listening in a mesmerised way to the performance by the tenor and orchestra. As the 1924 poetry slam nears to an end the host from Scotland attempts to conclude the evening but no one can hear him because the cheering is so loud and no one seems at all interested in listening to him anymore!

This is a victory Ruben should be immensely proud of, considering the intense rivalry taken place with himself and the German Lars Winserheinen. When competing to be crowned champion of poetry slam, there were so many extremely talented poets who could have won the contest quite easily if they had just experienced a touch of luck on this crest of a wave atmosphere regarding the connection with the audience on the final night of poetry slam along with the deciding judges. However, the crest of a wave was Ruben Edwards's to experience in going down to the wire upon winning the final when it came to defeating Lars Winserheinen for the title of poetry slam!

This other edition of Bruce Ismay is, without doubt, a future contender for poetry slam. He has taken the name to a new realm by displaying his poetic power on the stages he can call his own, with the originality of his performances. As all hope starts to appear to be totally lost for a certain J. Bruce Ismay on his quests through New York City with one thing and another. There is the appearance of this Canadian Bruce Ismay the poet, who appears with a completely different presence and personality. To make things even more interesting regarding these two namesakes, there are two individuals having recently arrived in New York City who have seen poet Bruce Ismay in performance.

This was at a well-known entertainment place not far from the central venues of Broadway, but still in the entertainment district of mid-town Manhattan. These individuals are two Spaniards, sent on a mission from Madrid, named Calero and Pedro Mendenez who thought they had seen someone from the past standing outside this particular entertainment place in Manhattan where there was an all-ticket poets' evening taking place. They decided to make their way over there, either to put their minds at rest it was not the person who they thought it was, or maybe they had gone over there to see if they had just seen a woman they thought was Francesca Draycott!

After a short walk across the street, they arrived at this traditional looking bar where this poets' evening was taking place. They were informed by the staff it was an all–ticket occasion and therefore they were not allowed in because of this.

However, after Pedro Mendenez had his say by telling them in his own classic Spanish way, they were stopping him spending a lot of money at the bar as he passionately informed a member of staff.

'You absolute fool of human being. Do you know how much money you have just stopped making its way to the bar? If you knew this, you would not have stood there and acted like a sergeant major and brought my entrance to a halt!'

The person he had addressed happened to be the event organiser who replied.

'Look, I don't know who on earth you think you are. For a start, you have not even got a ticket for the poets' evening. Seeing as though you have no conscience about producing a ticket upon entering the place, the night is an all-ticket anyway.'

After Pedro Menendez was informed by the event organiser of this he looked away in disbelief. He then glanced back at the organiser and said.

'Ticket? Who on earth would buy a ticket to get in there?' As the organiser was about to address him again, there was an ongoing commotion making its way towards the entrance of the place. Before the event organiser could even acknowledge properly what was going on, the arguing entourage hurtled past those assembled at the front doors like a herd of elephants in the Sahara! After this, the conversation between the event organiser, his staff, Pedro Mendenez and his right-hand man Calero came to an abrupt end as they all became part of the entourage as the commotion made its way outside!

In the ongoing upheaval, Pedro Mendenez and Calero had their lucky moment to get in the building as the path was clear to make an entrance to the poets' evening. Pedro Mendenez made a dash to get out of sight from anybody in his attempt to get into this entertaining bar, unfortunately for him, he went flying head first into the door, a movement resembling that of a ski jumper and knocked himself out! As his fellow Spanish colleague looked on, wondering what a waste of time it was all turning into.

-Chapter 10-

The Emergence of Benjamin Hartley

Former Titanic passenger, Benjamin Hartley, has now re-entered the frame, via another fiasco of an incident relating to his anti-social approach as well as his intolerant outlook on certain individuals he seems to run into in his human existence. This time he has gone one better and it is the German poet Lars Winserheinen with whom he has exchanged altercations with. The previous evening, in the later hours at poetry slam, he was involved in an incident with the runner-up poet after Winserheinen accidently spilt an alcoholic beverage over him at the Valentine Inn, in New York City where the 1924 poetry slam contest had been taking place throughout the evening.

The only reason Hartley was there in the first place, with his right-hand man, Archie Knox, was because Knox had directed them to the wrong venue. As dedicated as Knox is to the cause, considering his partnership with Hartley, he is not what he once was regarding his efficiency in decision making for any given situation. Becoming aware of this, Hartley is occasionally starting to take a second look at Knox as he wonders whether or not he has had his day in the realms terms of their professional acquaintance. Leading them to the wrong venue in Manhattan has not helped his cause, considering Hartley is now going to have to explain himself to his business colleagues for a no-show having turned up at the wrong place!

In the commotion the previous evening, Lars Winserheinen unfortunately tripped up and his beverage was spilt directly over Hartley's white shirt. In doing so, the red wine left Winserheinens wine glass with military precision, where Hartley replied.

'You absolute fool of a human being! What on earth do you think you are doing?'

Winserheinen was clearly more concerned about his fall together with the fact he had lost his glass of red wine. He looked up at Hartley, initially saying nothing. After a moment's pause, he said.

'Good evening. I am Herr Winserheinen. I am a poet from Berlin.'

This incensed Hartley he did not even receive an apology from the German as his white shirt was now looking more like the red carpet laid out for a high-class ceremony. It was at this moment Hartley struck back in classic upper class fashion shouting.

'You belong in a Berlin bar for the no hoper's, if not the nearest one! Now get back on the ship you travelled here on, and don't bother sailing over here again! You German idiot.'

In the midst of all this, Ruben Edwards has won poetry slam at the same venue. However, Hartley and Knox coincidently missed this part of the evening with Ruben, Anna, John Albert and Francesca Draycott enjoying the victory. Since Hartley and Knox had found their way to the wrong venue anyway, it was honestly not in their thoughts and is certainly not their priority to bother about the previous evening's entertainment. What a bizarre set of circumstances there would have been with Hartley and Knox walking in to see who they would have thought to be George Edwards standing there addressing the audience in New York with his poetry!

The next day following the victory for Ruben Edwards at poetry slam, just when things couldn't get any worse, Benjamin Hartley is in his office. He is now in quite good spirits after his encounter with the German and looking back on the evening he finds it funny. However, he nearly chokes on his tea after looking at the photograph of Ruben Edwards on the front of his newspaper. He crushes the newspaper, throwing it across the room in disgust, not even bothering to read it properly and not even recognising or realising it is not even George Edwards!

Not long after this, later on that day, Hartley bizarrely and coincidently notices Francesca Draycott taking a picture. It is an exciting moment considering he has not seen her since the night the Titanic sank. She is taking a photograph of Ruben and Anna standing outside a horse and stagecoach cab they are about to climb into. Hartley only sees her taking the picture and does not see Ruben. This is an intense moment with a defining but explosive atmosphere, with Benjamin Hartley now wondering whether or not he is better off sectioned in the nearest New York mental asylum! He scrambles away from the people near him when he realises it is her, with his right-hand man, Archie Knox, within close proximity.

'Do you know that woman? What is this building she has just made an exit from?' Hartley is hectically asking people!

On this occasion he misses her after running for the cab. Within this intense atmosphere Hartley is rejuvenated again after being mentally fixed on recovering the ancient scroll! Although he is unaware of what this historic writing actually is regarding the full in-depth knowledge of everything concerning this ancient manuscript.

This particular writing is a preserved map and with this you also need a certain magical key that opens a hidden door leading to a number of creatively detailed like labyrinths foretelling prophesies, where there is a hidden altar and church, out to the south east of Rome in Italy. The whole experience has now taken over him again and psychologically he is transfixed on recovering the ancient scroll with this intriguing key having now unintentionally taken command again!

Since first leaving his possession on board Titanic, if not left somewhere, the ancient scroll appears destined not to be with Benjamin Hartley. His sole desire has been to recover this ancient writing. However, as time has gone on and with the way he has settled into a new life in New York, he has gradually lost any interest in ever retrieving the historic map that is ultimately an ancient scroll. He has come to the realisation he is never going to regain ownership of this again, considering the circumstances of being unable to find George Edwards and Francesca Draycott. Since then, he has gone onto establish a construction company in New York City, taking his ventures down different entrepreneurial avenues. He pursues the wealth of success in his business dealings where, until now, he has honestly let the thought of this ancient writing go, in accepting he will never see it again and at the same time have no connection with the historical key.

Benjamin Hartley has now had another close encounter with who he thinks are a certain George Edwards and Francesca Draycott, yet once again these two particular individuals have made a great escape! However, he is not aware this is not George, it is Ruben Edwards! Once again, Francesca has slipped his net, so to speak, after another close encounter involving them both; with Francesca not even knowing Benjamin Hartley was in the vicinity anyway!! Hartley's agenda is now going to be clearly planned. He is now planning on tracking them down and finding his onetime possession he perceives as rightfully his, seen as though he paid a substantial amount of money for it, in what now seems an eternity ago!

Benjamin Hartley is now planning to recover the map on this ancient scroll starting first of all with him hiring someone to track them down, just so he knows one hundred per cent it is them and therefore confirming he has located their whereabouts in New York City. At first he considers himself and Archie Knox completing the required task at hand. However, he decides not to involve Knox because the whole circumstances surrounding the recovery of this ancient scroll are now becoming more like a military operation. He also takes a look at his right-hand man deciding it is best not to, considering his age and thinking he is not up to it.

His mind goes back to the night on board Titanic when Archie Knox could not even guard the first-class room and stay there, having left the door open when he decided to go and get a night cap. Therefore he decides this time it is best he plays a more behind the scenes role. Hartley still has an immense sense of respect for his Scottish right-hand man considering, the night Titanic sank, Knox was on the ship when it broke in half and he not only managed to survive the drag of the ship sinking into the north Atlantic, he miraculously swam out to safety and was pulled into a collapsible lifeboat nearby. Hartley privately admires Knox's great escape from the freezing ocean on the night of the disaster, but he thinks any major involvement in heading the operations here is now definitely not for Archie Knox, although the Titanic veteran will remain his assistant for the time-being.

Hartley now needs to know what is going on so his plan to recover the ancient map can be put into place. After this he hires undercover personnel to complete what needs to be completed in finding out the whereabouts of all concerned, not knowing Ruben Edwards , the man who is in company with Francesca Draycott, is not George Edwards. When at first viewing the pictures of those involved, he thinks it is George Edwards and he and Francesca have cashed in and sold the ancient scroll shouting.

'They've survived it!' In his rage, he throws all the photos past Knox in the office they are situated in, after clearly confirming it is them.

After a moment's thought, his hope is somehow they still have this historic scroll having scribed the drawings of a detailed map, if not he hopes the two of them will possibly know the whereabouts of this ancient drawing and writing if they have sold it. The worst case scenario for Hartley is Francesca has sold the ancient scroll, if this is the case there would then clearly be money not recoverable because she may have spent it. However, privately, Hartley would love her to still have the historic manuscript, considering what he has experienced to date! The quest is now taking place for everyone involved concerning this ancient map, with ultimately, the intriguing and mysterious key!

What Benjamin Hartley does not know is Francesca Draycott, her fiancé George Edwards at the time and her mother Vivienne, were sent from Italy where Vivienne and Francesca both have family descendants, back to where they resided in Southampton, England. When in Italy, they were asked to protect a certain historical key by missionaries with part of this mission being to travel across to America via England. Privately Francesca wants to keep the key close to her because it is not this item's financial value that intrigues her but something special that cannot be explained she feels for this beautiful and fascinating key.

As Benjamin Hartley is becoming more and more aware of the situation combined with the recent social rigmaroles having recently taken place in comparison with other social encounters, it appears psychologically the wheels seem to have started to come off. From what was becoming a prosperous time business-wise for Benjamin, with his rejuvenated air of confidence he had experienced, unfortunately things are genuinely going from bad to worse, considering all the circumstances of everything. Wherever he has turned up on the social scene in New York recently, he has just experienced some comical personality clash, whatever the occasion and wherever he may be. There is also another situation could be a lot better concerning Hartley's business contacts. Lately, when exchanging professional dialogue with his business associates during meetings, he appears to be getting very agitated and frustrated as soon as something does not go his way as far as what is regarded as normal human communication goes.

Business associates having established a very good working relationship with him are now starting to take a second look at him. In a business sense, everything that has worked for him recently in his career now seems to be on the road to nowhere, taking into account the atmosphere in some of the recent board meetings. Since his mind has been transfixed from where he was psychologically as a businessman to someone who is now concerned about nothing else but recovering this ancient scroll, he has completely lost all sense of reality within himself.

When Archie Knox attempts to resolve the situation by speaking to him, he just looks at him as if he is not there. Without doubt, the professional atmosphere between them that has been a force to be reckoned with at times, is now tailing off into no-man's–land! As Benjamin Hartley is waiting in his office for Knox to arrive, he is becoming slightly impatient as he pulls the office blinds slightly ajar to see if he is there, where he should be, parked up in the usual parking area assigned to his New York office. However, no car is there. Just before Hartley gives up on him and phones for another car to chauffer him to his desired location, he sees Knox driving towards the office building. As the car approaches the usual parking place, Archie Knox drives straight past it and pulls in at the wrong parking area a lot further down the street. Benjamin Hartley continues to look out of the window in dismay! He is now even more confused as to what is going on.

-Chapter 11-

A Night Out to Remember

As the euphoria associated with Ruben Edwards's victory at poetry slam is still in the air, he has planned a night out, along with fiancée Anna, John Albert and Francesca Draycott. It is early summer with a nice light summer's breeze blowing across New York City as the early evening sun shines brightly outside. The beep of a car horn is heard in the street below as the night out is ready to begin.

'Are you ready people? The taxi is here. Let's get out there and enjoy ourselves.' Ruben implies jubilantly.

There is an inspiring air of new beginnings as these exciting characters make their way to the waiting car outside of their apartments. With this change in the air atmosphere appearing to have descended onto their lives in New York, this night out coincides with a let's get away from it all feeling happening to be present.

After the glory of winning the title at poetry slam, there comes that time when the euphoric moment having been experienced and enjoyed passes. The fact of the matter is no one can stay in that moment forever but they can definitely go there again in achieving this success. There is an old saying with which we become familiar, time waits for no one. Here there is a presence of this life experience with the passing of the glory at poetry slam now in its own victorious part of time.

The night out has been arranged with the four of them going out to watch the New York Yankees who happen to be playing the Boston Red Sox. This has been built up to be one competitive and exciting encounter, considering the stature of the two baseball clubs along with the current strong form of the two sides. The rivalry of this fixture goes back quite a long way in baseball history. You just know when these two clubs play one another there is going to be a sense of occasion for this historic fixture. Ruben and Anna are going to be in the Boston Red Sox away end at the Yankee stadium while John and Francesca will be on the other side of the stadium with the home supporters. John Albert has always been a fan of the New York Yankees throughout his life and he appears to have also signed Francesca up as a fan, if this is the situation. If not, she clearly does not have a choice as far as the night out goes as John is her other half and clearly you would not think Francesca is going to end up in the away section supporting the Boston Red Sox with Ruben and Anna. Well, no one would think so anyway, considering the fixture!

Before the party makes their way to the Yankee stadium, the four of them are going to call at a few bars in Manhattan and soak up the atmosphere of the baseball fixture present throughout New York City. There is an intense expectancy and genuine excitement in the air throughout the city as the Yankee fans await the continuation of their historic rivalry with the Boston Red Sox. They are making their way to the ground with some people calling in at various locations throughout New York and experiencing the great atmosphere associated with this meeting of two of the greatest baseball teams in American history. At the stadium, the New York Yankees' coach is approaching the home ground and the fans gathered there create a euphoric cheer, knowing their team are about to arrive at the stadium to take on the Boston Red Sox. As the navy blue and white coach pulls in, it stops in line with the pathway to the players' entrance, there is an immense flashing of camera lights as the journalists start to picture the arrival of the team as the players step off the bus to enter the stadium. The moment has arrived for these players and everyone assembled to experience the sheer excitement of this historic baseball occasion on this early summer's evening.

Meanwhile, Ruben, Anna, John and Francesca are having a great time in Manhattan. They are having a few drinks before making their way to the stadium. The atmosphere is building throughout the city as the two great rivals prepare to play one another in this great baseball fixture which is generating even greater anticipation as the start of the match approaches. They all finish off their drinks, and then make their way out of the bar. As is usual in New York, they need to flag down a taxi. John Albert is the one who raises his hand to hail a taxi on the high street and one pulls up almost immediately. The four of them board the taxi and are greeted by a Jamaican taxi driver who says.

'Welcome to the car people. Where are we going to then?' He has a friendly and outgoing persona as he welcomes his guests to the vehicle.

'Hello, my friend. Can you please take us to the Yankee stadium? That's the place were going to.' Ruben replies to the driver with an upbeat tempo.

'Easy now Yankee boy! I used to play for the New York Mets.' The driver making an outgoing but comical response. After a moment's pause and short silence, he starts laughing with him 'I'm a New York Yankees fan as well. Good to meet you, my friend!' He says to Ruben. There is great laughter among everyone and a very comical atmosphere in the air as the driver has welcomed his four guests to the car.

'I'm actually a Boston Red Sox supporter. That is the place I am from. John Albert is the New York Yankees fan. He moved to Boston a few years ago.'

The taxi driver again responds enthusiastically.

'Albert boy. Easy now, Yankees boy back in town!'

'That's the one! Good to be back in town to see the Yankees play. It's been a few years now since I've been to see them at the Yankee stadium. I'm looking forward to it to be honest!' John Albert replies passionately. With everyone now laughing and appreciating the camaraderie of the Jamaican. The taxi drives off into the night and they are on their way to the Yankee stadium to see their teams play in this classic encounter!

They are now driving through the streets of New York towards the Yankee stadium on this glorious evening feeling a great sense of occasion as they approach the stadium for what is promising to be a truly competitive match. As the taxi starts to approach the stadium, the traffic is becoming slightly busier on the roads leading there. Many crowds are starting to congregate at various bars not far from the stadium. Thousands are making their way on foot as well with the pathways and roads leading to the arena at full capacity for the game.

With the traffic now almost coming to a halt, Ruben says to the others.

'I think we should get out now, seeing as though we are so close to the Yankee Stadium. What do you think people?'

'Yeah, let's go for it everyone. We are not that far away now' John replies.

'Time to leave the car then my friends. This is where the journey ends. You know it's good Yankee Stadium nearby!' As the driver joins the discussion.

All four of them exit the taxi as John Albert walks forward to the driver's window and asks him.

'How much do I owe you then.'

'Albert boy, call it one dollar ten.'

'Sure John replies' and pays the Jamaican taxi driver. Then they all say goodbye as the next part of the night begins.

They all start to walk over to the stadium and quickly join in the momentum of the crowd walking towards this great stadium. Euphoric singing by some fans has started to fill the air. With none of this four having been to a baseball match for some time, they do not know any of the new songs, especially Anna and Francesca. In fact, it is highly unlikely the ladies ever knew any of the songs anyway as they have never attended the baseball fixtures on a weekly basis before. Having said that, although John Albert has been to games before he is definitely not the type who has attended weekly baseball games to watch the New York Yankees. As he says to Ruben.

'Can you remember any of the songs from when you were at the games in Massachusetts?'

'Can I remember the songs, my friend? Albert, if I could not remember any of the songs from when I was at these games, I don't think I should be walking towards this stand to support the Boston Red Sox!' Ruben replies surprised.

With John Albert now looking at Ruben Edwards as if he was from another world, he competitively responds by saying.

'You have quite a good memory from those days when you were always at the games.' He continues. 'Good to see your both off to the other end of the stadium Ruben. Hopefully you can stay with the score. Just like you fluked your win at poetry slam' as the subtle competitor in John Albert is starting to show himself.

Ruben responds with a determined resilience.

'That was not a fluke! What planet are you on, making a comment like that. I thought you was starting to look like a one-trick pony after a few Shakespeare plays after the other.'

'Ruben, you can never call anyone who acts like me in Shakespeare classics. The poet is never the actor. The actors stage is more than any poetry reading could ever be when comparing those two stages with what is required to deliver a challenging performance!'

'Rubbish, you're talking absolute nonsense Albert. They are both totally different. I've never heard somebody come out with a comment more useless than that! The poet is the one with the creative power! This is your Yankee Stadium, Albert! The Boston Red Sox are going to record a memorable win here and show you how to play!' Ruben again responding with fighting spirit.

John Albert then senses the euphoric atmosphere he remembers from when he did go to the games; maybe his acting roles have taken their toll by psychologically exhausting him at times in his life. However, having said this, he has always been a really well-known actor, in being very talented at what he does. This acting adventure has already taken him from New York to Boston, Massachusetts, and back again as the dream lives on. This time at a night game on the playing fields of the Yankee stadium!

-Chapter 12-

Benjamin Hartley and Archie Knox meet Al Capone

Since Benjamin Hartley's campaign began to recover this ancient scroll from who he thinks has it, with those individuals being George Edwards and Francesca Draycott, he has not exactly succeeded with flying colours in the way he has gone about locating his onetime possession. Everything that could have gone against him in his pursuit l has done. His double act, with Archie Knox as his right-hand man, and their recovery quest has turned into a complete farce. They have only a general awareness of the situation, having not really made ground in achieving their ultimate goal of finding George and Francesca. After making a few lines of enquiry to little avail, Hartley has been informed on the social scene somebody form Chicago named Al Capone, could maybe locate this historic possession but at a substantial financial price.

He discusses the various options with Archie Knox and what is the best course of action to reclaim his long lost possession. At first he is extremely apprehensive about involving Al Capone and his associates in what is going on because he does not know them, considering the circumstances regarding the value of the ancient map. Hartley and Knox are running out of ideas. They have already involved other business associates in the search for the scroll but no one has succeeded yet in locating any of the people concerned in the matter.

They cannot locate Ruben, Anna, John, Francesca or the map in their search throughout New York City, even at the venues where Ruben is presenting his poetry on stage, accompanied by his fiancée Anna in the audience, as well as or the acting venues where John Albert takes to the stage. Francesca Draycott seems destined to remain unnoticed in the way that Benjamin Hartley cannot see her anywhere. Hartley and Knox always just miss them in their attempts to locate them in order to ask them the location of the historic possession.

After the discussions with Knox, it is starting to look as though Hartley has no choice but to involve Al Capone's searching experience and tactics with what is now looking more like a lost cause in finding anyone.

In the office of his New York business premises, Hartley says apprehensively to Knox.

'What if he steals it?'

'Well, it looks as though we have no choice, we can't get to them' Knox replies referring to Ruben, Anna, John and Francesca.

Hartley and Knox have a vague knowledge of a few things regarding those concerned but nothing definite. Initially, Benjamin Hartley actually thought Ruben Edwards was George Edwards, with part of him still adamant this is the case.

The fact Ruben is George's brother is an alarming thought for Benjamin Hartley and truly difficult to understand. Archie Knox looks over to Hartley who is now looking out of the window, seated in his office chair and says.

'They must have their residencies in different names to avoid anyone locating them. I don't know how they have managed to do it, but that's what it looks like.'

Benjamin Hartley swings around in his chair, looks at Knox and replies.

'Very well. It's time for me to get on the phone to this Al Capone.' After a moment's pause, he says in an apprehensive and comical way. 'Let's hope he doesn't start reading it' referring to the ancient scroll.

Benjamin Hartley dials the number been indirectly handed to him through an Al Capone associate, calling himself Larry, who has liaised with Archie Knox. They have both decided the best course of action is to involve Al Capone and his associates as they are now going nowhere fast in their pursuit of this map. Hartley is about to make a connection either going to see him reunited with this long lost map, or on the other hand, he quite simply might never see the treasured possession ever again, considering the circumstances.

The phone rings and is answered relatively quickly. The male who answers on the other end of the line says.

'Hello, this is Mr Capone's office. Speaking?'

Benjamin Hartley replies with in an unusually comfortable manner considering some of the people he is now involving.

'Hello, this is Benjamin Hartley speaking. My right-hand man, Archie Knox, has spoken with you previously about locating certain individuals. He was given this number.'

Al Capone's associate refers to his boss on another line by informing him.

'There's someone wanting to locate certain individuals.'

'You'll have to send him over. I don't do them over the phone. Book him in.' Al Capone replies.

The associate of Al Capone refers back to Benjamin Hartley in saying.

'Right then, Mr Hartley, can you come over for a meeting? Mr Capone would like to see you and discuss the situation with you. When can you make it?'

'I would be much obliged to come over for a meeting; I think that would be good. I can make it tomorrow at one pm.'

'See you tomorrow at one. It's the third floor directly facing the Empire State Building.' He then hangs up, which is how a phone call of this nature usually ends.

Benjamin Hartley on the other end of the line takes the phone away from his ear as he wonders whether or not he has just spoken to an ally, and also contemplates at the same time if he has just arranged his own downfall!

The next day arrives in New York as Hartley works his usual office hours at the helm of his construction company. Later on, he knows he has a very important meeting to attend concerning how an historic scroll he has not seen in many years could possibly be retrieved. He had almost given up on ever seeing it again. His enthusiasm for the recovery of this map is now rekindled and he has an optimistic outlook for a positive result. The day follows its usual course as far as business negotiations go, speaking to people by phone and company associates visiting the office to talk business.

Benjamin Hartley is excited about finding of the scroll because he has genuinely convinced himself Al Capone is now the man who can retrieve the map from George Edwards and Francesca Draycott. He is looking to the future in great spirits, thinking there is no way Francesca and her closest acquaintances could outwit this individual and his associates when it comes to them handing over the ancient map.

The car parks up as the moment to meet Al Capone has arrived. Archie Knox informs Benjamin Hartley his chauffer is waiting to take him to the meeting, where his new associate is waiting to find out why Hartley has asked to meet with this Chicago gangster, Al Capone. The journey to the meeting is a calm one, with Hartley resigning himself to the fact this is now his last ever chance to find George Edwards and Francesca Draycott and recover a lost possession he dearly desires.

He is not solely focused on actually finding them both; the situation is one where he thinks Francesca is the only person who knows what happened to this map, , possibly departing Titanic with the ancient scroll in her possession. This is the understanding of where Benjamin Hartley's thought process is at following his maze of life experiences on this recovery quest of this writing.

The car stops outside the office block. A man wearing a trilby, black coat and a defining pair of checked shoes walks over to the vehicle, where he makes a move for the door and says.

'Mr Hartley?'

As Benjamin Hartley looks at him in a surprised manner and replies.

'Yes.'

'Come in then. I'll walk you up to the office.' The man says.

Archie Knox attempts to get out of the car with Hartley but is told by this man who has met them.

'No, not you Mr. Just you as arranged. You'll have to wait in the car.' Informing Knox he will not, as he first thought, be attending the meeting.

They both walk up the steps to the building and through the double doors already open, as Hartley is informed.

'We won't be taking the lift. We're on the third floor. That's the office where you are going to be speaking to Mr Capone.'

As they arrive on the third floor, Hartley starts to look impatient as he is told to wait outside the office for a moment by somebody else. The man who has escorted Hartley there knocks on a black wooden door and walks in. He returns a few minutes later.

'You can go in now; Mr Capone is waiting for you. Please go in and walk straight into the office through the next set of doors.'

Hartley then stands up and hurries into the office, passing through a small cloakroom area before entering the main the office. He walks in and says in a very impatient manner.

'About bloody time. Now let's get on with business! I'm already pressed for time as it is.'

Seated in his office chair, his new business associate swings around drawing on his already lit cigar and says in a strong Chicago accent.

'Let me stop you there, Hartley! Now, the first thing I'll tell you is you don't walk into my office in that manner and you certainly don't speak to me like that either. Now get out of the office and come back in again in five minutes time, so we can start again.' At this point Hartley is stopped in his tracks as his impatience comes to a shuddering halt in the middle of the office. He looks at Al Capone in a slightly surprised manner saying.

'Very well then, I thought we were scheduled to get things going?'

Al Capone, with his smoking cigar, replies from his chair.

'Look Hartley, we seem to have got off to a bad start here. First of all you steamroller into the office without introducing yourself to me, then you start giving out your orders to me straight away. Now, get out of the office and go back to the waiting area. I'll show you all about getting things going Hartley! I've got some other moron, Pedro Mendenez to see after you as well.' As he presses a state of the art buzzer he has recently had fitted to his office desk.

Another associate of Al Capone's hurries into the room as he orders his new client out of the office.

'Hartley! Get back in the waiting area before you get sent back to the car!'

Hartley looks at Al Capone's associate in a disorientated way replying.

'Where has the other one gone who met me outside and escorted me up here? By the way, who are you all anyway?'

Angrily, Al Capone stands up looking at Hartley. As he makes his way over towards him via his wooden rectangular desk, the associate grabs hold of Hartley and escorts him back to the waiting area, closing the office door on the way out!

-Chapter 13-

Mid-town Broadway, Manhattan

In living the New York City dream, there is a place poet Ruben Edwards and actor John Albert have truly made their home in the creative and entertainment auditoriums in this historic part of Manhattan. Just like when they were fellow miners back in Boston, Massachusetts, they have journeyed together, although this time the journey is one of modesty to complete glory regarding the realisation of these dreams in their lives. As modest as this beginning was, they both arrived in a state where one can make it happen in the entertainment district, as far as New York City goes. These two both arrived full of hope, with a determined resilience to fulfil those destined dreams in this part of the world.

They made great progress in creating an awareness of their talents through making contacts at the right places in this great place of opportunity. This part of New York is really well known for musicals, shows, hotels and entertainment venues. Compared with Boston, where Ruben began his quest as a creative entertainer, the actual district and its vicinity are completely different from the entertainment district of Broadway. The place is larger in size regarding the entertainment industry and career opportunities. This area is the capital of the United States of America considering how many auditoriums there are situated along Broadway. In the bars, shows and musicals there is this energy of inspiration combined with an uplifting atmosphere on which all these entertainers can thrive in the buzz of this historic place!

When the poets take to the stage, there is a sense of a natural atmosphere the auditorium was built for them. It is the same for the musicians as well, with this sense these buildings are here for these creative individuals. When it comes to the acting venues, this same vibe exists when everyone has the experience the actual palladium was built for the acting world with the stage design and the interior architecture. The theatre-style places have a unique presence in the way they are designed for everyone as performers whether poets, musicians or actors.

Upon arriving in New York City, John Albert was immediately seeking opportunities as an actor because this part of the world demands a certain amount of earnings to cover the cost of living. The idea was for him to establish his acting roles over a certain amount of time ingoing from strength to strength. However, just like Ruben Edwards, he found his way to a reasonable place sooner than expected on his quest for decent acting roles. It all began when he gained the main part in the 'The Merchant of Venice' at the New York Palladium. This Shakespeare classic was chosen by the company concerned and John Albert had good luck with the audition because he has previously acted in the play and is therefore familiar with it.

John Albert is familiar with Shakespeare's plays and had good fortune when this role was advertised soon after he arrived in New York. This luck continued as his next acting adventure was again in a play by William Shakespeare, this time 'Macbeth', also at the Palladium. His role as 'Macbeth' was a challenging one since his previous role in 'The Merchant of Venice' was a completely different part. As Macbeth, he had to take his acting expertise to a different level in the way he displayed the character.

After acting in 'Macbeth' John Albert became a better all-round actor. This part was made for him in the way it took him to new heights as an actor in New York City. Before his latest role, he played one last part in a Shakespeare production of 'A Midsummer Night's Dream' by the same American company. This time it was the part of Nick Bottom and it brought his acting in the William Shakespeare productions to an end as he moved on confidently after achieving great success in these challenging acting roles. The few years he spent acting in these classic plays paved the way for him to establish a high-flying reputation at the New York Palladium.

John Albert's role he is currently working on in rehearsal is that of George Washington in a theatre production of a play called 'American Independence.' This is his first lead role since starring as Macbeth which established him more securely in his profession. The part of George Washington is the first in his acting career where he is being asked to play a great American leader and portray this to the audience. The role is the most demanding part he has had to play since Macbeth, in delivering a quality of leadership to his audiences as he plays the part of America's pioneer leader in the country's quest for independence. In the face of war, while fighting against the British red coats, John Albert will have to capture that belief to survive fighting for his country's freedom from the rule of King George III.

At the same time as this inspirational journey is taking place for him, his great friend Ruben Edwards is experiencing similar success on Broadway in Manhattan, with his victory of poetry slam having propelled him to new heights in his quest for poetic glory. The success of becoming New York's number one poet has also taken Ruben to a new realm, just like it did for John when playing Macbeth. They have taken part in one inspirational journey of creativity and entertainment since arriving in New York City. They are at the pinnacles of their professions; they have shown all the determined resilience required to succeed just like they did as miners back in Boston where it all started for them.

The next step for Ruben is to hopefully establish his career further by distributing his writings in published books. He could then go on to achieve even more with his poetry. He is going to pursue this avenue as the next adventure in his poetic career in order to complete what he set out to achieve. He has been assigned a publisher after his victory as a poet. There is always the other side of the coin with everything you can experience in life and it is no different for Ruben Edwards, if he is to become more psychologically focused on distributing his writings through publication. He knows he must not lose his creativity having made him what he is so far, however at the same time, he also realises his work has to be published following his poetry slam success. Destiny has now handed Ruben Edwards the opportunity of a lifetime to achieve this as he goes from strength to strength on his creative quest.

Not long has passed from when Ruben was awarded the trophy for poetry slam to when his chauffer driven car pulls up outside the central book shop in downtown Manhattan. The publication of Ruben Edwards's first anthology of his chosen poems is on the bookshelf in New York City. A private dream he has always had in his mind, even back in Boston, Massachusetts, is now becoming a reality in more ways than he thought and he just takes everything in his stride. Well, in more ways than one as he now has to make his way past the waiting crowd when walking into the book store. This dream of his creativity is one he has always known he could achieve one day, but had the conscience he could continue to work in different realms along the way, just as he did working with John Albert and the rest of the miners in Massachusetts.

Ruben steps out of the burgundy and black spoke wheeled car having now stopped directly outside the store where a crowd is waiting. With his fiancée Anna, he departs the car to a cheering crowd and they make their way over to the entrance in the early afternoon sunshine. Ruben stops to sign a few autographs as some of the crowd call him over.

One of the fans says to Ruben.

'When is the next anthology of poems out Ruben?'

'The next one? I've only just finished putting this one together. Are you sure you've read all these yet? The publishing company have only just put this one out,' he says, having a laugh with the lad.

'How do you mean? I thought you were working on the next one Ruben.' The younger fellow replies as an air of comedy is present.

With Ruben now wondering whether or not his enthusiasm for writing poetry has gone slightly crazy he says to the lad.

'I have many poems I could publish to be honest my friend but this is the first anthology of my poetry that is on the shelf just for now.'

The lad then puts his thumb up to Ruben and naturally understands people are not supposed to read too much of a poet's work too soon after one writing has been published. With the crowd still cheering outside the shop where Ruben has arrived for his signing session, he and the lad wish each other all the best as they now go their separate ways with the crowd starting to sing triumphantly!

Ruben and Anna walk towards the entrance of the book shop; the owner holds out his hand and greets them both.

'Welcome to Coliseums!'

'Thank you sir,' Ruben continues. 'Should be a good afternoon for everyone and maybe we can have a few victory drinks later tonight.' He responds celebratory. As there is a nice mild afternoon sun shining with a rejuvenating cool blustery breeze whisking by in Manhattan.

-Chapter 14-

The Quests of Those Involved

With Ruben Edwards now crowned the king of New York as a poet, considering the number of talented poets who competed and could have won the contest, winning poetry slam has to be regarded as an immense victory. It is also a success because of the way other poets inspired the crowds and were really liked by the people who listened to them throughout their creative journeys hoping to be crowned the poet King of New York. If this is an once-in-a-lifetime victory in New York City for Ruben Edwards, it is one where he is going to have to take a one day at a time way of thinking after being crowned the champion. You could say going on to defend the title is going to be a harder poetic experience, because of the intense competition there is to be crowned the champion. On the other hand, Ruben has accomplished what he set out to achieve in winning the contest against these competitive poets who all fancied their chances.

Lars Winserheinen wanted this title just as much as Ruben Edwards in the latter and final moments of the contest. The German was aware of the energetic presence of this fellow poet who had arrived from Boston, with the way he established himself on the New York poet scene and progressed to become the champion of poetry slam in the face of intense rivalry. Anna, his fiancée, has captured the moments in quite a beautiful way, being his lover as well as his photographer; she has also made good progress on the New York scene in promoting her photography work. They are living quite an enjoyable experience at this time as they are very down to earth, considering their New York experience, where they are having an inspirational time with their creative successes.

There has been another success story in New York where John Albert has established himself on the acting scene. His acting has taken shape in a much more productive way than it did when he was in Boston. In parallel with Ruben's achievements in New York, John has experienced the same realisation of one's dream in another creative way on stage, as an actor. They have both made really good progress in the sense having seen New York City take to them in a really inspirational way. They have fulfilled their destiny how things have happened on the poet scene and acting scene in New York, where they have both made great names for themselves.

Ruben Edwards has poetic strength in the way he connects with the audiences. You can really understand what he is talking about in his poems and the message he is communicating is clearly understood by his audience; his words speak to the people. The reaction of his audiences is a good indicator of the way he connects with them in a charismatic way.

John Albert has his own style with how he also connects with his audience. Firstly, he is standing on a different stage with his creativity being understood in his performance as an actor. He has his own vocal approach regarding the aura he displays when asserting his energy into his acting. He is able to play different parts in many varied productions giving him flexibility in when it comes to finding his next role. John finds his other life as an actor, just like Ruben does as a poet. When they were living in Boston, they worked in the day as a miner where it was important to show working resilience and it is this determination they both take to their stages as an actor and a poet.

Francesca Draycott has started to show an interest in becoming an actress herself. She has now informed John she thinks it is her time to shine; believing her time to take to the stage has now arrived. She has felt slightly unfulfilled when practising John Albert's scripts with him. She has told him this is just not enough for her. Francesca believes it is her turn to become established as an actress in New York the way John has achieved success in proving himself as an actor.

Meanwhile, Benjamin Hartley has started his quest to recover the map from Francesca Draycott who he believes has it in her possession. He has now become even more motivated about recovering the ancient scroll. Since he has become aware Francesca is residing in New York, after an encounter outside a theatre on Broadway in, Manhattan, he has become completely focused on finding the map and, if she has it, recover the ancient scroll from her. She narrowly escaped him without even knowing how close he was to her while boarding the horse and stagecoach with John Albert, Ruben Edwards and Anna. In the sheer pandemonium of New York City, Hartley thinks Ruben Edwards is his brother George. He is having flashbacks to various moments on board Titanic, not only how George Edwards and Francesca Draycott came onto the scene in the first place, but the ultimate moment he is remembering is when he actually placed the ancient scroll on a deck bench when on board Titanic.

The reason he is having these particular visions of this moment is because to his recollection, since then he has not seen the map. On this occasion right-hand man Archie Knox wondered off after having a few beverages and this took his mind of the ancient writing at this moment in time.

Benjamin Hartley is starting to wonder why everything went so horribly wrong in his connection with George Edwards and Francesca Dracut after he was introduced to them a few years previously at a village gathering near Rome in Italy. There is something he cannot explain about how badly things continued to go from bad to worse from the moment he noticed them on board Titanic. It could be argued this was the defining moment he sensed something was wrong, if you could define one pivotal moment in their connections as people.

When referring to the ancient scroll, Hartley appears to embark on a wild goose chase in the sense he is, without doubt, destined not to retain possession of this historic map going off past experiences. In his private thoughts of thinking about what happened where and when in his life, he is struggling to comprehend how things tailed off so badly in his keeping of this ancient writing, considering the idea of buying this historic map at an auction in a village near Rome, was to keep a financial security for himself and his future. Even more mysteriously the ancient scroll should not have been present at the auction Hartley attended in the first place.

There are moments when Archie Knox tries his best to enlighten Hartley from day one the connection with George Edwards and Francesca Draycott was just not meant to be. He also tries to explain to him he simply has to acknowledge maybe the ancient scroll is not supposed to be with him and this is just the way things have taken their course in his life experiences. Knox ultimately advises Hartley he should not waste too much time in thinking about things having been and gone since there are circumstances he cannot change when it comes to his experience and previous connection with George and Francesca.

In the midst of all the drama with Benjamin Hartley's now resilient quest to recover this long lost map, there is another person who has become aware of the situation through a couple of social occurrences and meetings in New York City. This individual is Chicago criminal Al Capone, who has been present on a couple of occasions when comical pandemonium has broken out at the bars where everyone concerned has been assembled. On the night when Hartley met German poet Lars Winserheinen when there was the unfortunate wine spilling incident, Al Capone was present on this occasion when the situation took place.

Being how he is, he naturally wondered what was going in the commotion, something he is no stranger to himself when considering his business dealings throughout the United States.

On this social occasion in conjunction with a competitive atmosphere concerning what was taking place with Benjamin Hartley and Lars Winserheinen, Al Capone took an interest in knowing who they were, considering he regards himself to be a social type of person regarding his reputation in America. This incident, along with the other meetings, has led Al Capone to the point where he has become conscious of what is going on and has made enquires with his associates throughout New York City as to who these individuals happen to be.

In the weeks following this brief encounter between Benjamin Hartley, Lars Winserheinen and Al Capone, the path is now set for them to become familiar with one another on the business and social scene in New York. Al Capone informs a number of his associates about the situation, how he has become aware of these certain individuals who seem to have appeared on the scene at the same time. He himself has returned to New York City to take care of his business dealings. He can sense something about Hartley and the German he has now gained a slight interest in, but he does not know what it is.

The fact of the matter is he likes to know who is who and what is going on because he has a number of business contacts throughout New York. He is always looking out for new business associates regarding his business infrastructure. If they seem the right type of person: when referring to the concept of business from his point of view. After he witnessed Hartley and Winserheinen in the bar area together, he instantly took a keen interest in who they were, considering he experienced being socially surprised by them because they looked more like two boxers about to have a fight in Madison Square Garden, when encountering one another in mid-town Manhattan!

New York is going from bad to worse for Lars Winserheinen as his defeat to Ruben Edwards is now sinking in. It was another close call, in again not winning poetry slam. There could be a danger Winserheinen will become accustomed to defeat in this annual poetry slam contest if he does not land the title next year! This creative contest is becoming a really well-known event hosted at various venues throughout Broadway in Manhattan. It is becoming even more competitive each year, so you would imagine it is going to become even more difficult for the German to win his desired trophy and become the king of New York on his quest.

Lars Winserheinen has to be given credit for his efforts so far in his contribution to the creative scene around New York City, considering he has travelled from Germany on his poetic quest to be recognised in the United States of America. He could not have gone any closer to winning this poetry slam title in the year he managed to get the runners-up plaque, being beaten by Ruben Edwards in the final. From his point of view, he now has to become a stronger poet in the way he responds after losing the final encounter this way. This is Lars Winserheinen's biggest test of stature as his quest now becomes one where he has to overcome another final defeat in this latest experience as a poet!

- Chapter 15-

The Car Chase to New York Harbour through to the Boats

As the recovery mission of the ancient map begins, Benjamin Hartley and Archie Knox both in black top hats and overcoats see Ruben Edwards in the street as the humid early evening descends on New York; this is where he comes into contact with Benjamin Hartley face-to-face for the first time. Ruben does not have a clue who he is, with Hartley clearly thinking he has finally met George Edwards again tells him.

'George, we meet again! Thankfully not in that no hoper of a bar like last time! Comedy is mixed with intensity throughout the encounter. Unusually the thunder and lightning strike again as Ruben Edwards is within the vicinity of Benjamin Hartley, just like there was when Hartley observed the cab pull away, driving off with Ruben, Anna and Francesca on-board, with Benjamin Hartley slightly looking up at the sky meaning lightning has struck again! As the heavens open and the rain starts gushing down, it gives Ruben a lucky moment to quickly depart the scene with Hartley and Knox looking up at the sky transfixed!

After this attempt by Benjamin Hartley and Archie Knox to gather information from Ruben Edwards, Ruben quickly manages to escape his would-be captors and returns to the high-rise apartments he shares with fiancée Anna, John Albert and Francesca Draycott. Ruben gets back to the residency. He ascends the lift to the top floor and frantically knocks on the door of John and Francesca's apartment. John Albert is not in as Francesca answers the door. Ruben asks her who this Benjamin Hartley is. Francesca does not want to believe what she is hearing. She tells Ruben they must both do their best to get away from Hartley and Knox. Another escape is required! The commotion has started! Hartley and Al Capone both want the historic map. Cars are heard pulling up outside the apartment where all four of these creative individuals live. The map hunters have done their research in knowing their residency. Ruben and Francesca both grab what they can in the panic of their escape.

'Quick! We need to get away. They've found us Francesca. Looks like the fire escape at the rear of the apartment.' Hastily Ruben and Francesca make a dash for freedom along the corridor! Ruben opens the doors of the fire escape. They carefully descend the black and sturdy metal stairs. Thankfully making no noise and at the same time not alerting anybody's attention.

They make it to Ruben's dark burgundy car. He inserts the key into the door of the vehicle, where he quietly pulls up the handle and gets in the car. Ruben keeps low on the seat as he reaches across and lets Francesca in! They have managed to get in the car with one of the entourage in close proximity and standing a few yards away from his vehicle. Shockingly he notices them! The chase has started in the streets of New York City.

Hartley's initial hope of recovering this historic map or being informed of its whereabouts is replaced by a resignation to the fact they might have sold it. However, he still holds a slight hope Francesca has kept it. Hartley is astonished when he is informed by Knox Ruben is George Edwards's brother. He responds in classical upper-class fashion.

'What a categorical disgrace! He belongs with the no hoper's as well!' Al Capone and the mob are on the scene as Ruben and Francesca are escaping! After everyone running through the apartment as if it has turned into some sort of high-rise military assault course, the realisation Ruben and Francesca have escaped down the fire escape is now in full flow! Al Capone and his henchmen follow as some hurry down the stairs of the apartment and some down the fire escape where they quickly get back into their cars. In the meantime,

Hartley partnering Knox have returned to their vehicle slightly ahead of Al Capone and co as they have set off in pursuit of the escaping pair. Also slightly ahead of the rest of the pursuing pack is the car that was nearest to the one Ruben and Francesca have escaped in. There is not much time at all from when the alarm is sounded about the fleeing pair to when the streets of New York have turned into the United States Grand Prix!

The car chase through New York is in full swing with Ruben Edwards pressing his foot on the accelerator and steering the car with immense assertiveness as he attempts to escape the pursuits of Al Capone and his entourage along with Benjamin Hartley, who is in pursuit with Archie Knox, in this intense drama of a car chase. There is even more pressure on Ruben concerning the fact he does not even know where he is going! There is understandably a lot more driving expectation than usual required from him to manoeuvre this automobile through the streets and out of the sight of the vehicle cavalry chasing them in this hectic encounter. After negotiating a few New York streets, Ruben has turned into some sort of Grand Prix driver considering the way he is driving the car, not only through the streets of Manhattan but to the standard he is taking the corners in his determined attempt to escape with Francesca Draycott, who is seated beside him hoping for the best!

Fate now hands them a lucky break in their attempt to escape! The driver of the first car in pursuit slightly loses control of the steering wheel. Now out of control, the front wheel of the car ends up catching a wooden beam balanced on a skip and being used for pushing up a wheelbarrow in building construction work taking place nearby. With two of Al Capone's associates in the car, the vehicle pulls a dramatic wheelie and travels a fair distance down the street after knocking all the scaffolding down. Eventually the car crashes on its side and is therefore out of the pursuit!

The following car does even worse than the one in front with the driver of this vehicle also losing control of his automobile. This car ends up driving out of control where it is driven up two wooden beams placed against a skip. It then takes off into the air, looking as though it has two stuntmen on board and eventually crash-lands in the next skip that is situated on the street. As this particular automobile is now also out of the pursuit, the driver turns to his accomplice and says.

'It's not my car.'

'I know. I can tell.' His associate replies. The accomplice tries to open the passenger door but it will not open because of the skip. He then says in a comical way.

'Looks like the sunroof!' With the construction site now looking more like a demolition job!

As the momentum of the car chase continues, Ruben Edwards's vehicle smashes through the middle of two harbour gates, where the car takes off into the night sky upon departing the quayside and eventually splashes into New York harbour, just to the side of the Mauritania that is docked there! Due to the momentum of the car chase, the third and fourth cars follow Ruben's vehicle off the side of the harbour. These cars have a similar destiny to their predecessors in the sense they take off into the New York air where there are dramatic engine like revs as all cars depart the quayside!

One vehicle dramatically ends up on the bridge of the Mauritania via another construction site that the car ascends in the momentum of the drama with the captain and his crew thankfully not in there, after the car smashes into it upon landing. As the driver and passenger somehow survive unharmed, they depart the car on the bridge of the ocean liner.

The driver throws the car keys and says to one of the crew who is stood outside the door of the bridge.

'Keep the car!' As they hurry and make their way of the ship.

The other automobile splash lands next to where Ruben Edwards's car has entered the water, with the drivers and passengers dramatically jumping out in mid air! Just like Ruben and Francesca previously, having also luckily been driving convertibles!

Hartley and Knox descend the harbour steps in quick pursuit of Ruben and Francesca, who have just escaped from a now-sinking car. They have boarded a tourist steam boat in the hope of escaping their pursuers: Benjamin Hartley, Archie Knox and Al Capone's entourage. Luckily they have boarded this boat just before it left for the Statue of Liberty with a boat full of tourists eagerly anticipating their visit to Liberty Island. Hartley and Knox descend the concrete harbour stairs but just miss the boat. Now losing patience with his right-hand man after Knox tells him to calm down, Hartley grabs hold of him and agonisingly says.

'Could you please stop advising me all the time! There are moments when I think we both should have stayed on board Titanic!' Looking a bit disappointed in his business partner, this is the first time Archie Knox loses all faith in Benjamin Hartley. Not only as his right-hand man and employee but also their working existence in general. At this point, Hartley experiences a moment's rejuvenation.

'Look Archie! There's a rowing boat!'

Now with a bit of daylight between them, so to speak, even though night has descended, the tourist steam boat Ruben and Francesca are aboard heads off to Liberty Island. Realising how lucky they have been to escape, for now anyway, they have a few moments peace to get their breath back, but only for a short time. However, the never-say-die spirit of

Benjamin Hartley is now being put to the test as two of Al Capone's drivers are swimming out of the harbour. Al Capone stands there and asks.

'Where's the car?'

At this moment, Benjamin Hartley looks over at them and says to Archie Knox.

'What an absolute debacle!'

Even if his quest to recover the ancient scroll is now bordering on complete insanity, Benjamin Hartley has noticed a rowing boat in close proximity to the harbour. He orders Archie Knox to quickly untie the ropes and row it out with him, which they do in quite good time as the tourist steam boat is not travelling fast and is still in sight. The pursuit is on again!

Hartley initially takes responsibility of the rowing boat with Knox navigating the best way he can to stay in line with the route being initiated by the steamboat. The rowing boat starts to make progress, in the sense it is going in the right direction. After tirelessly putting his heart and soul into gaining water on the steamboat, Hartley now needs an actual rowing partner to continue at the speed they are travelling across the New York Bay. Knox now takes up the other oar and they are quickly rowing in unison in their pursuit of the steamboat. They start to make immense progress in terms of closing the distance between their rowing boat and the steamboat. Hartley and Knox start to pick up speed, rowing across the harbour looking more like a coxless pair in an Olympic final going for a gold medal!

As Ruben and Francesca are stepping off the steam boat onto Liberty Island, Ruben just about notices the rowing boat closing in on where they have landed. He quickly informs Francesca, who is by his side as they depart the tourist steam boat and hurry onto the island. After making what looks like the best come-back in rowing history, Hartley thinks the historic map is now within his grasp for the first time in years! As he stands up to step off the rowing boat, agonisingly, he loses his footing and ends up dramatically falling into New York Bay close by to the Island! His moment of a lifetime to reclaim this precious writing has again passed him by in what was his closest call to be reunited with the ancient scroll.

Knox shouts to Hartley, trying his best to assist him and keep him believing in himself.

'Benjamin, this way! You are facing the wrong way. I am over here.' Archie Knox having now climbed out of the boat and is standing on the island.

Hartley responds to Knox from the water in what is now a farcical scene.

'To be honest, there's nothing left to believe in!' As he swims out of the water drenched, Hartley knows he has just gone within touching distance of the ancient map for the first time since being on board Titanic.

Ruben and Francesca start to run off because Ruben has seen Hartley with Knox arriving at Liberty Island.

'Quick, let's get out of sight. I think we've got a good chance of getting away here. They both seem to be in disarray!' Ruben implies.

Francesca grabs hold of Ruben as she says, in a resilient manner.

'Where are you going?'

Ruben has just seen Hartley take a tumble after making an immense rowing journey across New York Bay. He is quickly thinking what to do next. He wonders for a second whether or not Francesca has now lost the plot and what she is about to recommend to escape Hartley! However, this is not the case. She says.

'Ruben, over here! All these people are walking away from this steamboat we have just departed with the crew as well. We have to go back in this!' Francesca has now suggested to Ruben they take the steamboat and abandon everybody in leaving them on Liberty Island. Ruben looks at her, pauses for a second and says.

'What do you mean? I cannot work one!'

'Just get in the thing and push the leaver forward! We need to get back over there.' Francesca persuasively replies. She is now desperate to escape considering the dynamic duo are within the vicinity.

After he has had a few seconds to think about the whole situation, Ruben responds passionately.

'Come on then Francesca. This steamboat is going back!'

-Chapter-16-

New York Hospital

The crowds, as well as a police presence, gather around New York harbour quayside in the midst of car headlights following the recent events having now passed, including a number of cars going off the harbour and into the water with another one ending up in the bridge of the Mauritania via a scaffolding construction!

As all this is taking place Ruben Edwards has managed to negotiate the Hudson River at the helm of the steamboat. With Francesca Draycott, they have managed to courageously escape the pursuits of Benjamin Hartley and Archie Knox that for the time have subsided. Both now wounded, they are in immediate need of medical attention. They are suffering a number of injuries received in the pandemonium of fleeing their pursuers including Al Capone's entourage.

After departing in the tourist steamboat that had harboured at Liberty Island, the vessel continues to be successfully navigated downstream, not that far from New York harbour. Ruben notices a concrete staircase in the distance where he presses down on the lever with the steam boat gradually coming to a stop. There is a gushing of water against the harbour wall. They both step onto the concrete and carefully make their way up onto the lamp lit street. Luckily, they have now made it to land again!

Ruben and Francesca need hospital attention concerning a number of injuries they have picked up during a hectic night. Fortunately a local resident is making his way to a motor vehicle as both Ruben and Francesca are seeking much needed assistance in getting to the nearest hospital. Francesca hastily calls to the man.

'Mr … please wait,'

'Could you please take us to New York hospital?' Ruben asks. We are in desperate need of medical attention, we are injured.'

'I have a few injuries and I honestly can't walk for much longer because the pain is worsening. This is Ruben, could you please helps us.' Francesca says.

The man seated in his car, is just about to turn his steering wheel and drive off into the night. He looks out of the window at them both as he says.

'Sure, get in.'

In her hand, Francesca has a holdall safely containing a precious key securely kept in a case. She has managed to keep her possessions!

Upon arriving at the hospital, the man who has driven Ruben and Francesca there jumps out. He opens the car door for them. He helps them make their way to the entrance. Four nurses hurry towards them and quickly grab hold of two stretchers on wheels. .

'I have an agonising ankle injury. My arm is in pain. There are cuts and pains I can feel as well. Ruben has a bad head injury.' Francesca explains as they are helping them onto the stretchers. Shortly after the nurses take their personal details.

'Good evening, I am the Sister. Thank you for all your information. We are now going to wheel you off to the correctly designated medical area. Here you will both be examined by the correct doctor.'

'You are both lucky considering how quickly you can be attended to. The hectic hospital is usually quiet.' Another nurse reassuringly comments.

'I just thought that to be honest. There's an unusual calm in the hospital.' Francesca replies.

Ruben and Francesca are exhausted following the pandemonium in which they have been involved throughout the night. They are both lying calmly on their stretchers and at last find some peace in the medical like aroma of the hospital ward away from everything previously happened. When they ask about the man who drove them to the hospital and helped them in, the nurses have no idea what they are both talking about, having not seen anyone. Francesca informs them.

'There was a man who kindly drove us here and helped us both to the entrance of the hospital.' It appears the nurses did not see the man who she is taking about.

'Sorry I did not see anybody as we came rushing over to assist you.' One of the nurses replies.

With everyone appearing slightly confused, Ruben adds in a comical manner.

'He must have vanished then, like a ghost! We didn't even have the chance to thank him!'

'You were lucky tonight; thankfully he was there and managed to drive you straight here.' One of the other nurses comments. There is a relieved atmosphere in the air with everyone now starting to look slightly confused as well. None of the nurses have any idea what they are both talking about having not seen anyone. Shortly after this conversation the nurses pull up the stretcher bars. The doctor has arrived on the ward to begin both medical examinations. Ruben is wheeled away for his medical examination by the doctor. He goes before Francesca because he has an injury needing immediate assistance. Ruben is slightly dazed looking up at the passing lights and seems to be lapsing into unconsciousness but the doctor says.

'Ruben, are you there? We are now going to x-ray your head injuries.'

'Yeah, I'm still here. I nearly fell asleep. If not, I've just nearly died!' Ruben replies to the doctor amusingly as he regains consciousness.'

A little over half an hour passes as the doctor returns from studying the x-rays.

'Ruben, after examining you, the injury is not that serious regarding a cranium injury. The affected graze is not a particular type of wound regarding a cutting of the tissue. Although I recommend a bandage to secure and protect the area I have examined.' The doctor continues. 'Again you have been lucky, this type of injury could have been worse. After examining your cranium the tissue does not need stitching as I first thought. One of the nurses is going to come over here and bandage you well. Please do now rest. The worst of the ordeal is over.'

'Thank you doctor, I fully appreciate that. To be honest, I am looking forward to having a rest. It has been a really long and eventful day.' Ruben replies in a graceful manner.

Francesca is then wheeled into the ward by the nurse who is attending to her. She is next to see the doctor and has a bad ankle injury sustained from when unfortunately falling over on it escaping the pursuit of Benjamin Hartley and Archie Knox on Liberty Island. Along with this she has an arm injury requiring examining. About another half an hour passes.

Having been examined by the doctor Francesca is informed by him she has been lucky as well.

'You have twisted it badly. It has clearly made impact with the surface you fell over on. However you have been fortunate. You have not had a break in the ankle. The arm is not broken either. This has been confirmed by referring to your x-rays.' Francesca looks back at the doctor and says.

'Thank you, I thought it was broken the amount of pain I'm in. Things could have quite clearly been a lot worse.'

'True, however please try not to worry. Like Ruben, the worst of the ordeal is over. The pain should have eased now due to the medication taking effect. If you have any further complaints, please do refer to one of the on duty nurses.'

Both Ruben and Francesca have a few cuts as well as muscular strains that are going to need time to heal. They are again seen to quite quickly by the nurses attending to them both. Following the doctor's examinations, Ruben and Francesca are wheeled back to their designated ward where they both hope to make a full recovery from their physical and psychological experiences throughout the duration of the evening. In the ward, they are placed next to one another so they can now rest. They look at one another and do not even say anything, as if to say what an experience that was!

As the doctor considers their injuries regarding the situation, he contemplates the best course of action. This being whether or not they need further examinations the following day. He thinks it is best to keep an eye on them both considering their medical situation. He tells them.

'For precaution we have decided we are going to keep you both in. This is for your own health and safety. You have nothing to worry about. However, we have to consider your best interests. We are going to check on both of your conditions for at least the next forty eight hours. The idea here is you can be discharged with our safe knowledge, knowing you are both good to leave.'

Francesca's mother, Vivienne, is informed of the news regarding Ruben and Francesca via a telephone call from the hospital in New York. She is made aware they have both escaped the pursuits of various individuals and straight away she can sense it is something to do with the ancient scroll.

After the phone call Vivienne is with Molly Brown where she turns to her and says.

'What on earth is the girl going to get up to next? I knew she should have stayed here with me working in the souvenir shop. I wonder what has happened up there.'

'Is that Benjamin Hartley and Archie Knox anything to do with this? I can remember the surprise encounter we had with them on board the Titanic. This sounds like him all over again!' Molly replies, looking at Vivienne in a slightly suspicious way.

After dramatically escaping this once-in-a-lifetime experience via New York hospital, Ruben and Francesca are reunited with their other halves who were unaware about what had been happening with how Ruben Edwards and Francesca Draycott ended up getting involved in this dramatic amphibious chase. At the time, John Albert was in his dressing room at the New York Palladium, awaiting Francesca's arrival. His usual routine of practising his lines with Francesca quite clearly did not take place on this particular occasion because of the unforeseen circumstances.

While waiting for her to arrive he actually delayed the start of the show so she would not miss the play in which he was about to debut and perform in 'American Independence.' As the crowd at the Palladium were starting to look around and wondered what was going on, John Albert was told by the production manager he would have to go out on stage and get on with it, which in the end was a good decision considering the evenings escapades, since Francesca was nowhere to be seen, being involved in the pursuit of the century hurtling through the streets of New York at the time and onto the harbour.

The following day Ruben's family members arrive at New York hospital as well after making the journey from Boston as the whole drama turns into a bit of a family gathering for all the wrong reasons since they are all at the hospital, having escaped a number of incidents that would not have been out of place in the actual New York palladium itself! In a way, what happens signals the beginning of the end of the tenancy in New York City where not long after leaving the hospital, they decide to move back to Boston, Massachusetts.

Benjamin Hartley and co manage to escape the pursuit of the New York police in the sheer pandemonium of the previous events. How all of them have escaped is quite bizarre considering three cars are now docked on the bottom of New York harbour after driving through the harbour gates and at the same time looking more like three car boats with another one ending up on the Mauritania. During the car chase, Al Capone lost five of his cars as two more of the entourage's cars were written off due to them crashing into scaffolding in the middle of the pursuit. It was quite a costly adventure that came to an end with him having five fewer cars in comparison to what he started with at the beginning of the day.

Once again, Benjamin Hartley's pursuit of the historic map was one truly magnificent failure of a wild goose chase. It was, without doubt, an indefinite waste of his valuable time considering he did not achieve anything again. With this latest attempt and recovery mission now almost extinct, Hartley must surely now be questioning his adequacy in reclaiming this historic scroll. He seems to be doomed every time he comes anywhere near the thing or when he has any kind of involvement concerning recovering the map. Considering he purchased the ancient scroll for quite a high price, anyone would have thought by now, he has considered whether or not he should have bothered in the first place.

Mysteriously, Francesca's experience with the ancient scroll is quite similar considering it seems to cause her nothing but sheer mayhem regarding all her experiences relating to this extremely valuable ancient writing. However, the defining difference between them is Francesca Draycott has an intriguing key in her possession and in a peculiar way this is what comforts her.

-Chapter 17-

The Handing Over and the End of the Road

As Ruben, Anna, John and Francesca make their way to the arch shaped and open double doors of the hospital exit area; it represents the completion of their escape from New York harbour to a place of sanctuary at New York hospital as a nice breeze blows in. After being involved in this dramatic pursuit through New York City never witnessed before, considering the drama that took place when escaping in not only the cars but the boats too, there is an atmosphere of relief they have managed to flee their pursuers. The medical attention both Ruben Edwards and Francesca Draycott required has now been given and the worst is over, considering how badly they were injured during their escapades through New York City.

Ruben is reunited with Anna after a medical representative had previously informed her he had been kept in the hospital due to his injuries so the medical staff could keep an eye on his condition. As John Albert and Francesca Draycott have also been reunited with one another in the hospital on the same ward an unusual calm has descended over the pandemonium of everyone's dramatic experiences for the time being. After narrowly missing out on thinking he was recovering the historic map, Benjamin Hartley must be now wondering what on earth he has to do to recover this ancient scroll.

As these four people return to their apartments in New York after another extremely eventful experience in their lives, there is talk of returning to Boston, Massachusetts, where maybe living will be safer, considering every Tom, Dick and Harry now seem to be on their case in pursuit of the ancient scroll. This historic map has now become the writing they would all like as well considering how Benjamin Hartley, Archie Knox, Al Capone and his entourage have all become interested in gaining possession of the ancient scroll.

The whole situation has become ridiculously out of hand when it comes to the safety of not only Francesca Draycott but also John Albert, Ruben Edwards and Anna, considering everyone is aware of everyone contemplating the situation in New York City. Benjamin Hartley is still dismayed at the situation where, no matter what anyone advises him about who Ruben Edwards is, he continues to be convinced this certain individual is George Edwards! He is in a way not listening to Archie Knox when he informs him this individual is Ruben Edwards and not who he thinks it is. Benjamin Hartley is adamant Ruben is George Edwards!

Maybe the time has come for Ruben, Anna, John and Francesca to return to Boston, Massachusetts because of all the dramatic happenings. Maybe they have lived the dream in experiencing Broadway, Manhattan in New York City. In a way, they have achieved what they set out to accomplish on all their quests as individuals as well, but there is clearly the challenge to maintain this success of winning for as long as possible, the poet of Ruben Edwards could be at his peak around this time. It is an experience he could possibly not achieve again because of the nature of the other poets' creativity and the energy of other performers, as well as being recognised in New York City as the number one poet.

John Albert is in the same boat of success as far as being at some sort of pinnacle in his career goes, where continuing would be in the best interests of John Albert the actor to maintain this success throughout New York City, considering how fickle the acting business is, especially at the Broadway theatres throughout this entertaining district. This same concept is true as well for Ruben Edwards knowing how fickle it can be for poets in the way they can be no longer seen as number one, just as much as they have persevered in putting their heart and soul into reaching their goals and succeeding.

Francesca and Anna have also found their home when they think about where they are in their careers. Francesca Draycott has started to perform on stage in Manhattan at Broadway's theatres where she is really looking like a natural in her new found adventure as an actress. John Albert is beginning to look a little apprehensive when he is about to act on stage with her, considering he has always been the acting focus of the two of them. Their partnership has quite clearly taken on a new dynamic in the way John Albert now has a new presence in the form of his fiancée. It is no longer just about John Albert and Francesca Draycott practising his lines for his forthcoming performances. Francesca is now fundamentally part of this acting extravagance in their existence.

Anna has been an extremely inspirational presence for Ruben Edwards during the successful times in his life, not just inspiring him as a poet but as his lover as well in their own romance. There have been times of modesty back in their home state of Boston, Massachusetts, when Ruben was working as a miner by day in the physically and psychologically demanding mining industry. Even back then both Ruben and Anna experienced an air of optimism with hope for the future as people.

They have arrived, just around the corner from the apartments where both couples live in this residential area in New York close to the district of Broadway, Manhattan. They pay the taxi driver through his window after leaving the vehicle on a road adjoining to where they live on what is a quiet evening so far. Upon walking a short distance along the road where their apartment residency is located, in a matter of seconds they have been surrounded! Many people have appeared, not just from the side of the road but they have stepped out of the cars parked there as well! There are even a large number of these people all dressed the same in black clothing, some in bowler hats and some wearing trilbies, standing looking down on them from the steel staircases of the apartments, all being armed as well. The four of them immediately stop in the middle of the street wondering what on earth is going on. The calm night on their way home has now turned into one of danger. Whoever these people are, they know who they are! They have been located … Ruben, Anna, John Albert and Francesca Draycott are about to find out who they are!

As they look forward down the street, they see a car approaching with headlights shining, lighting up the street at the same time. As the car approaches, these four residents are under the vehicle spotlight on this mild New York evening. The car door is opened by someone who also exits the vehicle via the front passenger seat of the car. Everyone concerned is about to get their answers regarding what is going on, including the individual who has just stepped out of the car that has pulled up. Every single person on the street, wherever they are, gives the impression of an extremely professional like exercise the way they have appeared in unison. The only people unaware of what is going on are Ruben, Anna, John and Francesca. The man walks forward where all four of them can clearly see who it is. He is flanked by two other fellow individuals. It is Al Capone!

He looks at the four of them and smiles. Then in a classic Chicago accent he begins to address them.

'What an exciting time it has been for everyone concerned, not just over the past few days but we've had quite an exciting time going back a few good months now! There are two things I'm not happy with though about the other night. The first is I've lost five cars in the grand prix we had through nearly every street of Manhattan! One car has ended up on a skip not far from here I can't get back now with another crushed under quite a bit of scaffolding. One of the other cars I'm definitely not going to get back because it went through a harbour gate, off the edge of the harbour and landed on a ship! I don't expect to see that again along with the other two that turned into car-boats as well; they sank when they went off the harbour, no thanks to the two of you who escaped when we all turned up at the apartments!' He says with a sense of comedy in the air. The four individuals he is addressing look at him and do not say anything in response to the joke he has just had with them.

Al Capone is now laughing to himself as he seems very proud of his joke about one of his cars now being on the Mauritania and two others being on the bottom of New York harbour, parked next to Ruben Edwards's automobile. He continues to address the four of them in going onto say.

'My drivers are OK, along with the other passengers, even though they all had quite an entertaining experience. The thing is though … One of you has now got something I want and if you let me have it, we can call it straight for the other night.' At this point, all four of them continue to look at him as none of them say anything after he has spoken to them because they probably fear the consequences of even responding to this individual who has now well and truly caught up with them as they all stand on a New York street!

As a deadly silence descends on the gathering underway in the middle of the street, Al Capone again addresses his listeners as he has not yet got the response he is looking for.

'Well then hello. Is anybody home over there? I do believe I have just been extremely diplomatic and informative in what I have had to say. I can't remember anyone saying anything unless I'm going deaf.' The shuffle of his entourage accompanies Al Capone's final demand for answers. The four are now on their last warning as they have made their presence felt as well. They are standing at many angles within the vicinity of the street. Somebody needs to say something!

A few more seconds pass in the street but it is at this moment Francesca steps forward. She speaks with a calm and polite tone of voice considering the circumstances.

'Wait. I have what you want. I have it here … It is the ancient scroll you are here for!' As she pulls the historic writing in its articulate holder out of her pocket!

Al Capone smiles with a look of delight, considering he knows he has now completed what he set out to do in finding Francesca and the historic writing.

'That's a very nice sight, Miss Francesca Draycott. We've put a lot of hard work into finding you and this ancient scroll. I think I've been on a bit of a wild goose chase at times with that Hartley.' He then raises his hand and moves it down to the side, signalling to his entourage to stand back at the same time.

At this point Francesca looks slightly disappointed because he even knows her name as well as addressing her by her surname. She also knows it is officially the end of the road regarding her affinity with the precious writing as she now walks over to him to hand the ancient scroll over.

'Wait!' Al Capone declares as he tells her to stop. He then says. 'Stay where you are Francesca. I'll come to you. That's how it works here.'

Francesca then steps back as she is looking quite surprised at now being part of the official street procedure. Al Capone walks over to her as she holds an historic looking cylinder holder safeguarding the precious writing in her hand. He holds out his own hand where Francesca Draycott hands over the articulate possession containing the ancient scroll.

At this point Al Capone looks at her and says.

'Thank you.' He then nods his head in a respectful way because he knows she never sold these historic possessions whereas in comparison, it is now his ultimate plan to do so.

-Chapter 18-

Back in Massachusetts

With everyone now back in Boston, Massachusetts, after an extravagant experience and residency in New York City, there is a changing of the guard aura in the air that seems to have arrived in the state concerning the adventure. Upon returning here after spending a few years in New York City, all four of them have lived a life experience and this seems more like double the amount of time considering a number of unforeseen events happening to take place when living there in Manhattan. Francesca and her mother are now ready to move on again in this comical, but truly exciting existence. It is not one of them plans to move to a new area, just like that. The situations happening to occur seem to be unpredictable in the sense that, after a certain amount of time; there is a desire to move on atmosphere descends on one of them.

Apart from Humphrey Draycott's extravagant musical experience. If it is not Vivienne who is ready for another place, it is Francesca who is considering escaping her mother and father! Throughout this time in their lives, for whatever reason, this is just how things are meant to be. Upon returning there is an air of departure from Boston, Francesca Draycott experiences, as she is now considering leaving the place for good. At first, her mother decides her daughter has gone insane as she tries to stop her packing up as well as departing in telling her.

'Francesca, you have found your career working in the hotel souvenir shop.'

Francesca looks at her mother, completely disinterested in being non-respondent concerning what she has just said. Vivienne might as well have just spoken to her in Dutch

Urdu regarding her silence and lack of enthusiasm about continuing to work in the hotel souvenir shop. Not only is she completely bored to death of working there, she is now tiring of her mother's continued advice. She is even planning on escaping from her because her mother's control and dominance is worse than it ever has been, considering the recent drama regarding what has happened in New York.

However, Francesca Draycott and John Albert decide it is best for both of them to re-locate and start again somewhere else after a dramatic experience in their lives, to say the least. They say some happenings in life bring you closer and in a way this is what has happened here. With all the pandemonium of everything they have recently experienced, there is an insouciant air of freedom now existing which has enlightened them both regarding they are now destined to leave Boston as well. Privately, John has started to question Francesca's inner being. He is wondering what on earth is going on. He is questioning why she is so attached to this ancient scroll and intriguing magical key seeing as though other people have tried to take possession of them since she first set eyes on them. He is also questioning why she did not at least consider selling these valuable possessions considering the experiences she appears to encounter. He is slightly bemused as to how she has this key in the first place anyway. John and Francesca have mysteriously never really spoken about how this happened. There is a presence of subtle comedy involving the whole situation regarding John Albert, Francesca Draycott, this historic key and the ancient scroll.

This part of everyone's life culminates with John and Francesca ultimately deciding to leave Boston with her concerned mother in the following year of 1925 after Humphrey Draycott informs them he has found them somewhere else to live, as this happens to coincide well with their present situation. Vivienne has surprisingly convinced Francesca she is better off with her, considering the dramatic happenings in her daughter's life to date. Vivienne has accepted her term as manageress of the hotel's restaurant has now concluded with her daughter's desire to move on from Boston. She has also reluctantly accepted Francesca's destiny is not at the hotel's souvenir shop with Francesca telling her mother she now feels like resigning rather than working there. This discussion Vivienne has with her daughter is quite an alarming one, considering Francesca informs her mother maybe she is better off in the local cemetery rather than working at the hotel's souvenir shop for the rest of her days in her own comical way.

Her mother informs her close friend Molly Brown she is going to have to move on with her daughter. Vivienne is now even more adamant Francesca needs her by her side because of the extravagant and intense life events she has experienced. Francesca hands her resignation to Molly Brown and thanks her for the employment opportunity she gave her by saying.

'Thank you Molly, for the therapeutic type of employment you gave me here. It took my mind off so many things early on. That was a really nice time. However, after returning from New York, it honestly might as well be another place, because I think it is time to settle somewhere else again.' Hopefully, the reason Francesca does not want to work there any more is nothing to do with the fact hotel owner Molly Brown, has had a framed painting of herself placed outside the shop!

The taxi is heard approaching the entrance to the hotel, where Francesca and her mother are on their way to departing for the train station. They start to make their way through the archway of the marble-floored hotel entrance. There is a slightly subdued but immensely thankful atmosphere as Molly Brown walks through the hotel with them. This is the women who in a way rescued them both from New York City in 1922 when Vivienne needed an escape from the place relating to where she was working because her reality had become not the most desirable. The atmosphere is mixed because both Vivienne and

Francesca are truly grateful for the way Molly offered them an alternate place to rediscover their own lives in what had become financial turmoil for everyone concerned, considering the lifestyle to which they were once accustomed to with Humphrey Draycott's music career. However, this is an experience they both came through and survived, in every sense of the word. Throughout this time, poetic justice took place as well with Humphrey Draycott establishing himself as one of the musical names in the United States and currently on tour again.

At the hotel entrance, where all three of them are walking out to meet the approaching taxi on a fine summer's evening, there is a man making his way towards the hotel in the sun like glow of this beautiful evening. Ruben is arriving to say goodbye. At first, no one sees him approaching the departure area as the luggage begins to be loaded into the waiting taxi for Vivienne and Francesca to head off into the setting sun of the Boston skyline. After already saying their goodbyes to Molly, the dynamic duo both climb into the taxi and inform the driver they are going to the local train station.

At the same time, Ruben is still on his way to the hotel entrance area, unaware of the departing taxi, where he is in a world of his own walking towards the porte-cochere; the car is slowly driving down. The car approaches him in conjunction with the particular path he is heading in when Francesca notices him. She calmly asks the driver to pull over so she can get out and speak to him. At first, Francesca pulls down the window as she asks.

'Ruben, where are you going?'

Rather surprised at how Francesca has called him, he replies.

'I thought you was over there, I must have been miles away' as Francesca opens the taxi door and she steps out of the car to speak to Ruben for what will be the last time.

Their journey over the past three-and-a-half years has been an extravagant one to say the least in summarising things. Their meeting was one where a sequence of events continued to happen culminating with Francesca Draycott being in Boston, Massachusetts with her mother Vivienne where Francesca was destined to also meet her future husband, John Albert. Vivienne, a heartbroken woman because of her loss of wealth during and after the Titanic disaster, ended up in New York City with her husband and daughter who found it incredibly funny they had become modest in comparison to how they used to live. Privately, Francesca was a young woman who felt bereavement due to the passing of her fiancé, George Edwards, during the allied advance to victory during the culmination of World War I and therefore also experienced her own heartache during the challenging experience. Her meeting with John Albert, as well as Ruben Edwards was a saving grace because this was how things were meant to be in the hectic life experiences of Francesca Draycott.

Francesca stands with her mother, looks at Ruben, for what they can sense is the last time. They know they were supposed to meet one another around the time they did in their lives to cure Francesca's sorrow with the passing of George Edwards, where she met John Albert at the same moment. In a poetic manner and being a great friend, Ruben became a cure for the bereavement and heartache Francesca had suffered in her young life. In return, she was the strongest of allies with Ruben when it came to him going one step further as a poet.

Ruben, Anna, John and Francesca all moved to New York City where, in a way, Ruben conquered America because New York is the most well-renowned place for poets. With Francesca there, she was part of the psychological dynamic supporting Ruben at times through this great friendship. As Ruben looks around, he notices his long-time friend and creative ally John Albert is not there. He looks at Francesca and says.

'John Albert, where is he? I nearly missed him. I'm probably never going to see him again.'

'I am meeting him at the train station. He is coming from the house. We have planned to meet this way because we are travelling to the train station from different directions.' Francesca replies.

Ruben is now looking a bit puzzled as he is thinking the meeting arrangements seem quite bizarre considering they are leaving Boston and heading off into the sunset to make a new life in another state. He says to Francesca.

'That seems a bit peculiar why you are not both departing from here together? I would have liked to have said goodbye to John as well. He has been a close friend over the years in everything we've achieved.'

Francesca explains to Ruben everything is all right as she reassures him.

'Don't worry about it, Ruben. He's probably forgotten you were coming over here to say goodbye. He said he had many things to complete, packing his belongings away. I think he just wanted to pack up everything on his own when it came to his possessions. With one thing and another, I think he just wanted to have a moment reminiscing about what he has achieved as an actor in Boston, Massachusetts and New York City as well.'

Ruben now looks even more confused regarding the situation with John Albert and wonders why he is not there as arranged regarding his departure. He is slightly concerned why John packed up everything on his own seeing as though he has always been a great team player. He asks Francesca.

'Is everything all right? Is he ok regarding moving?'

Again Francesca reassures Ruben, in saying.

'Look Ruben, I've just told you, you're not to worry about him. He's perfectly fine. Once I get him on the train, you won't have to give him another thought.'

Ruben smiles in an accepting manner regarding the way his lifetime's friendship and partnership appears to have now disembarked with John Albert. It also looks like his alliance with Francesca Draycott is now over as well. After climbing back into the waiting taxi, Francesca looks out of the window and says to Ruben.

'Goodbye Ruben. Take care and good luck with everything!'

-Chapter 19-

The Ending of Stepping off the Carpathia

Ruben is now back in Boston, Massachusetts. He is on stage and about to begin his latest poem titled 'Inspiration.' Francesca and her mother are now leaving Boston as the train approaches the station. There is a peculiar kind of atmosphere in the air, not only at the Wagon and Stagecoach where Ruben has always read his work, but in and around this particular part of Boston as well. Ruben looks out to the audience. However, the usually exciting Ruben Edwards can sense the presence of the end of an era. He is still good at capturing the imagination of the familiar Boston crowd but there is something a little subdued about him the home crowd are not used to. Has Ruben Edwards passed his peak? Is this the beginning of the twilight or is he showing the audience his uniqueness as a poet? He begins.

Inspiration

Take a look round; ask the questions you want,
In time you know, because the answers they show,
We waste precious time, but soon were'll see the sign,
Were'll take a look around and make things better,

What happens next, that is up to you and me,
Whatever's around the corner, that's what were'll live to see,
We all try to find,
A better place and happier peace of mind

But Saturday and Sunday,
They won't wait for us,
Because there's too much of everything,

With too much fuss

Take a look around; ask the questions you want,
In time you know, because the answers they show,
We waste precious time, but soon were'll see the sign,
We'll take a look around and make things better,

What happens next, that is up to you and me,
Whatever's around the corner, that's what were'll live to see,
We all try to find to find,
A better place and happier peace of mind.

But Saturday and Sunday,
They won't wait for us,
Because there's too much of everything,
With too much fuss.

Saturday and Sunday,
They won't wait for us,
Because there's too much of everything,
With too much fuss.

The poem ends and there is a euphoric response from the home crowd, just like there always has been when Ruben Edwards reads his work to the people of this part of the world. They know, on this particular occasion, this lad has lived through some experiences on his eventful adventure throughout his life. He is back in his home town with his latest poem symbolising everything he has lived over the past few years. The poem from Ruben's perception is not only about his experience about moving away from Boston, Massachusetts and heading to New York City with Anna, John and Francesca, but it is about returning somewhere in your life, not only geographically but in a way you cannot explain; something becoming brand new again in the way you move on in your life in a naturally pleasant way, mysteriously having no heartache involved as well as being inspirational in the sense there is hope for the future and time waits for no one.

Francesca and her mother arrive at the train station where a new dawning awaits them as they step out of the cab, gathering their belongings with the driver assisting them as he helps them on their way. After they pay him, he wishes them all the best as they walk over to the station where they are destined to leave Boston and journey to a new place in their lives. It is a really nice summer's evening with a cool breeze in the air; it is the wind of change, considering there are people now going their separate ways.

Vivienne goes over to the ticket office where she buys herself and Francesca their one-way tickets, signalling the end of yet another adventure in their unpredictable existence. As the sun shines on her face, Francesca says to her mother in a placid manner.

'Mother, thank you for everything over the past few years, considering all that has happened. Thank you for being there for me as we have lived our experiences.'

Francesca's mother looks at her surprised because she has never said anything like this to her before. She looks away as the train pulls in, as if to say, I know what you mean you don't have to say anything.

As Francesca and her mother step on the train, they just miss the sound of a car hurrying towards the station. It breaks to a halt, just stopping in time before hitting a water trough that is situated outside. Thankfully, the vehicle has now stopped and not driven through the train station ticket office as well as driving through the actual train itself! Benjamin Hartley and Archie Knox have arrived. How on earth they have found their way to

Boston, Massachusetts, has to be regarded as a mystery. How they are so tantalisingly close to Francesca Draycott and her mother, Vivienne, is anybody's guess as far as Benjamin Hartley is concerned.

Benjamin Hartley is now trying to open the car door, for some bizarre reason it has jammed shut in the commotion. He shouts out with all the vocal power in his being.

'Open!!!!' But yet again, the car door remains shut. Meanwhile, Archie Knox is trying to communicate with him from the passenger seat but to no avail. Hartley, now psychologically isolated in his own mind, turns to the door, lifts his feet and legs up and frantically kicks the door off in a moment of escapism! The door flies past the ticket office where the employee who is seated there looks out of the window, wondering what on earth is going on!

Hartley quickly climbs out of the car and has to remember where he is for a few seconds. He hears the sound of the train's departure and it is now looking like he is once again going to miss out on the recovery of the ancient scroll he so painstakingly desires. Ironically, he has been informed by Al Capone he did not retrieve this historic map from Francesca Draycott. He rushes through the ticket office with Archie Knox. He is stopped by ticket guards at the station. Not even being able to communicate in the sheer mayhem of the experience. He wrestles his way off them. Benjamin Hartley, followed by Archie Knox, runs back out of the ticket office. They turn right towards the other end of the station where there are horses having been taken away from their stagecoach ferrying duties, along with other horses assembled and knotted there.

With the owners all mysteriously assembled in the bar within the vicinity, Hartley stops for a moment to decide which horse to mount for what will now be his pursuit of the train about to leave the station. He quickly realises the stagecoach horses are not inclined to be mounted and hurries to untie a brown chestnut-coloured horse. For some reason, the horse looks at him as if this is the one supposed to share the quest with him! Hartley mounts the horse, where for some reason they are luckily in unison regarding the atmosphere of horse and rider. He quickly takes command of the horse's reigns and turns around towards the direction of the platform as well as the train. They begin to trot around the side of the station, past a sign that says, 'No Horses On Platform!'

Hartley does not even see the sign. Even if he did, it would not make any difference whatsoever in the now extreme circumstances of his insane but resilient pursuit concerning the recovery of the ancient scroll. As the horse now canters around the side of the station towards the train with Hartley in the saddle, they are following a pathway that is taking them to the edge of the platform. Wasting no time at all, they approach the edge of the ramp-shaped platform. Hartley grabs the reigns and urges the horse up the platform shouting.

'Gallop, horse. Come on, horse!' The horse gallops up onto the train station as they continue at pace along the platform, eventually managing to compete with the speed of the train where at the same time they are catching up with it as well. Hartley and this brown chestnut-coloured horse have now taken to one another like two Grand National winners! They might as well be galloping along the final furlong at Aintree or Cheltenham Racecourse! Has Benjamin Hartley's moment arrived? Is he now about to board the train, like a hero from the Wild West, as he now thinks he can finally recover the historic map from Francesca Draycott?

Hartley looks up at the train and there she is! Francesca Draycott, sitting by the window. Agonisingly, he starts shouting.

'Francesca Draycott, the ancient scroll!' But she does not even hear him and just sits there in a calm way looking forward out of the window in completely the opposite direction from where Benjamin Hartley is shouting from while he is riding at speed alongside the train. Now courageously attempting to grab hold of a rail at the end of the carriage in which Francesca is seated as the locomotive increases in speed slightly, he is again tantalisingly as close as he could be to a showdown with her to find out where the ancient scroll is that he regards as his!

Hartley is still caught in two minds whether or not to grab hold of the rail where he could board the train in an extremely unusual fashion. He is now risking his life, considering how fast the horse is galloping after the train. Dramatically, he pulls the reigns and the horse comes to a halt, having luckily noticed the road running out in front of him! The horse stops quite quickly, taking Benjamin Hartley slightly by surprise during the drama of the experience. Hartley loses control of the reigns as he is thrown over the head of the horse! The horse stops just in time in front of the edge of a ravine, throwing Hartley over the front. He desperately tries to hold onto the reins but to no avail. Now, in serious danger after being thrown off the edge of the ravine in the momentum of the experience, he grabs hold of some vines on a tree that luckily has broken his fall over the edge of an extremely high ravine!

After desperately getting as close as ever to being in the presence of Francesca Draycott and after trying to recover the ancient scroll, he might as well now be a million miles away from her as he has turned into Boston's very own version of Tarzan, if not Indiana Jones! Descending via the vines that have ultimately cushioned his landing, he glides down the ravine towards a running river that is flowing under a train bridge that the locomotive has now started to travel across. Benjamin Hartley was as close as he could ever be to asking Francesca about the ancient scroll as he takes part in this dramatic experience! Upon a splash landing into the river Hartley is lucky enough to survive it, considering the depth of the water and how the vine tree has glided his descent of the ravine!

With the train heading off into the sunset with Francesca and her mother on board, this must surely symbolise the end of Benjamin Hartley's adventure after what is, without doubt, another hopeless quest to recover the now long-lost ancient scroll, as far as he is concerned. On the train, Francesca looks out of the window. She has a beautiful historic key in her coat that she dearly treasures and with which she shares an affinity. With Benjamin Hartley luckily surviving his extravagant experience, he hurries out of the water and looks up the ravine as he shouts.

'Archie Knox, where are you? You silly old fool! How on earth do I climb back up this?'

Hartley does not receive a response from Knox because he is nowhere to be seen. He is still making his way towards the ravine following the railroad that the train has just travelled along. As Archie Knox is once again making an immense effort to assist Benjamin Hartley with the latest mess he has managed to get himself into, there is now another disastrous occurrence that takes place. At the moment Benjamin Hartley steps back, he slips and loses his footing as he starts sliding into the fast-flowing stream that is rushing under the railroad bridge. He now has to swim into the unison of the stream as well as making sure that he stays above the water where he does so in quite an amphibious way!

Archie Knox now arrives at the edge of the ravine where he looks down as he calls to his long-time friend and business partner.

'Benjamin! Are you there? I cannot see you!' Archie cannot see Benjamin Hartley because he has started to sail downstream; caught up in the pleasantly flowing current that is now transporting him out of the state, as he starts to look like he is enjoying himself! Meanwhile, in New York, Larry, Al Capone's assistant, rushes into the office. He has just been to have the ancient map and holder Francesca Draycott handed over valued!

'Mr Capone, I've got some bad news!' Sitting at his desk, Al Capone drops the newspaper from his face as he says in a surprised manner.

'Bad what????'

Francesca Draycott has done the unthinkable in handing Al Capone a fake that he thought was the most expensive possession that he had ever set eyes on! She had an ancient scroll made with a map of somewhere imaginary detailed in preparation for ever needing to regarding the protection of the intriguing and mysterious key. Thankfully, Ruben, Anna, John and Francesca all departed New York City in good time before this copy was taken to be valued.

As all of this is happening, there is one more man that cannot be forgotten! John Albert has pulled in at a Boston train station where he hurries out of his car and into the waiting room.

'Francesca my dear, are you there?' He calls, but he receives no reply as there is no one in the waiting room. He rushes out to the platform area calling. 'Francesca, where are you? I am here!' Again, he receives no reply because the platform is empty! He hurries back to the waiting room area and asks the ticket lady in the office if she has seen two women, in describing Francesca and Vivienne. After looking at his rail purchase the ticket lady informs him.

'This is not the train station you should be at. You have turned up at the wrong one!'

Meanwhile, the two of them continue journeying on the locomotive. Where initially, Francesca does not even remember they were supposed to meet him, thinking they would meet on the train anyway in their seats! Once again, the beautiful spiritual presence of the magical key and the existence of the intriguing ancient scroll have mysteriously taken command, as Francesca and her mother Vivienne are travelling off into the sunset with John Albert now hopefully on the next train as another adventure and drama is already in motion!

Bibliography

Encyclopedia Titanica: Titanic Facts, History and Biography, [1996] Available from: <http:// www.encyclopedia-titanica.org: [2018].

New York City – Wikipedia, the free encyclopedia, [2018] Available from: <http://en.wikipedia.org/wiki/New_York_City: [2018].

Carpathia And The Rescue – Titanic-Titanic.com, [November 1990] Available from: <www.titanic-titanic.com/carpathia.shtml: [2018].

RMS Carpathia – The Great Ocean Liners, [1999] Available from: <http:// www.thegreatoceanliners.com/carpthia.html: [2018].

Bruce Ismay (Character) - IMDb, [1990] Available from: <http:// www.imdb.com/character/ch0002359: [2018].

Titanic's Captain Edward John Smith, [1990] Available from: <http://titanic-titanic.com/captain_smith.shtml: [2018].

Charles Herbert Lightoller : Titanic Second Officer, [1996] Available from <https://www.encyclopedia-titanica.org/titanic-survivor/charles-herbert-lightoller.html: [2018].

Arthur Godfrey Peuchen : Titanic Survivor, [1996] Available from <https://www.encyclopedia-titanica.org/titanic-survivor/arthur-godfrey-peuchen.html: [2018].

TIP | United States Senate Inquiry | Report | Outline – Titanic, [1999] Available from: <http:// www.titanicinquiry.org/org/USInq/USReport/AminqRep01.ph: [2018].

The Titanic Disaster Aftermath, and the Internet, [March/April 2001] Available from: <http:// www.infinite-energy.com/iemagazine/issue36/titanic.html: [2018].

World War I | Facts & History | Britannica.com, [2010] Available from: <https://www.britannica.com/event/World-War-I: [2018].

Hospital Ship Britannic, [2000] Available from: <http://www.hospitalshipbritannic.com: [2007].

Hospital Ship - Hospital Ship HMHS Britannic, [1997] Available from: <http://hmhsbritannic.weebly.com/hospital-ship.html: [January 2018].

The Lusitania Resource: Lusitania Passengers & Crew, [2005] Available from: <http://www.rmslusitania.info: [2018].

Titanic and Other White Star Line Ships, [1994] Available from: <http://www.titanic-whitestarships.com/: [2018].

RMS Olympic, Sister Ship to Titanic, [1994] Available from: < http://www.titanic-whitestarships.com/Olympic_1911.htm: [2018].

RMS Olympic Troop ship – Ships and navies – Great War Forum, [2014] Available from: <http://1914-1918.invisionzone.com/forums/index.php?/topic/210104-rms-olympic-troop-ship/: [2018].

The Battle of the Somme, 1916 – Great War, [1998] Available from: <www.greatwar.co.uk/battles/somme-1916: [2018].

Smith Called Back Half-Filled Boats, [1996] Available from: <https://www.encyclopedia-titanica.org/smith-called-back-half-filled-boats: [2018].

The Great War - 1914-1918 – Battles of the Western Front 1914-18, [1998] Available from; <http://www.greatwar.co.uk/battles/: [1998].

Molly Brown (Margaret Tobin): Titanic Survivor Biography, [1996] Available from; <https://www.encyclopedia-titanica.org/titanic-survivor/molly-brown.html: [2018].

Boston – Wikipedia, the free encyclopedia, [2018] Available from; <https://en.wikipedia.org/wiki/Boston: [2018].

Al Capone – IMDb, [1990] Available from; <www.imdb.com/name/nm0135330: [2018].

The Empire State Building – Visit New York's Observation Deck, [2018] Available from <http://www.esbnyc.com/: [2018].

Broadway (Manhattan) – Wikipedia, the free encyclopedia, [2018] Available from <https://en.wikipedia.org/wiki/Broadway...Manhattan: [2018].

The Merchant of Venice (2004) – IMDb, [1990] Available from <http://www.imdb.com/title/tt0379889: [2018].

Macbeth (2015) – IMDb, [1990] Available from <http://www.imdb.com/title/tt2884018/: [2018].

A Midsummer Night's Dream (1999) – IMDb, [1990] Available from <http://www.imdb.com/title/tt0140379/: [2018].

American War of Independence (1775-1782), [2003] Available from <http://www.historyofwar.org/articles/wars_american_independence.html: [2003].

New York Hospital – Wikipedia, the free encyclopedia, [2018] Available from <https://en.wikipedia.org/wiki/New_York_Hospital: [2018].

Giacomo Puccini – Encyclopedia Britannica, [2018] Available from <https://www.britannica.com/biography/Giacomo-Puccini: [2018].

Printed in Great Britain
by Amazon